The Detectives

The Detectives

Short Stories of Closed Rooms,
Dead People, and Unusual Detectives

David Davis

BOOKLOGIX®
Alpharetta, Georgia

ISBN: 978-1-6653-0654-6 - Paperback
ISBN: 978-1-6653-0655-3 - Hardcover
eISBN: 978-1-6653-0656-0 - eBook

Library of Congress Control Number: 2023912401

⊗This paper meets the requirements of ANSI/NISO Z39.48-1992 (Permanence of Paper)

071823

For Kathy and Elizabeth.

Contents

Hurricane House   1
The River   79
Yuma Mystery   92
At the Baptist Student Union   123
Dark and Bloody Ground   166
The Round One   187

Acknowledgments   *207*

Hurricane House

Monday

It was 12:05 p.m. The phone rang.

"Statistics. This is Sara FitzGerald."

"This is Director Struber."

"Yes, sir."

"You're a sworn agent, right?"

"Yes, sir. But I'm assigned to Criminal Statistics."

"Well, temporary change in assignment. I have a case for you. A request has come in from the Chief of Police in Carolina Beach."

"Isn't that in the Jacksonville district, sir?"

"Yeah, but they are all tied up with that drug smuggling investigation near the Marine base. Passed the request on up to Raleigh. We're pretty thin ourselves, so I'm pulling you away from your computer and putting you in the field."

"I have a Friday deadline for that analysis you requested on the geo-spatial correspondence between property crime and socio-economic status in North Carolina."

"I can wait on that. It's just going to show that poor people steal from poor people. This shouldn't take long anyway. Chief of Police says they have a 'locked room' murder like on some TV show. Probably just means they don't know what they're doing. Asked us to send Sherlock Holmes. I guess they will have to settle for Agatha Christie. I'll clear it with your Special Agent in Charge."

She decided not to say anything about Sherlock Holmes being a fictional character and Agatha Christie being a real woman who wrote murder mysteries. At age twenty-six, Sara really didn't want to be compared to little old lady Miss Marple. So, she kept her mouth shut.

"You're to meet a Detective Douglas Butts, B-U-T-T-S, at the police substation at the municipal docks. Directions are to take two lefts just past the Baptist church in Carolina Beach, park by the docks, and look for the sign. Usual mileage and travel expenses will be approved. And you're going to have to go out on their boat, so you probably want to change before you leave."

"Yes, sir."

"Show them how it's done, Special Agent."

"Yes, sir."

And the phone call was over. North Carolina State Bureau of Investigation Special Agent Sara FitzGerald hung up the phone, saved all the files on her computer, took the small black backpack she used as a purse out of her desk drawer, and headed down to the restricted parking area for agents. There, she unlocked the trunk of her personal car, a two-year-old, dark-blue Toyota Corolla, and pulled out her suitcase "go-bag." She then lifted the mat and pressboard cover of the spare tire well, revealing a hidden compartment she had installed herself. Unlocking the metal frame holding down a steel gun case, she lifted out the case, closed the trunk, and headed back into the SBI office building.

Using her badge to avoid the metal detectors at the guard station, she headed to the Ladies' room on the floor where most of the Special Agents in the Raleigh headquarters had their offices. Since most of them were men, there was less chance of being disturbed here than on her Criminal Statistics office floor. Plopping her suitcase and gun case on the mandatory pull-down diaper changing table, she shed her light blue "business-casual" dress and flat-heeled leather shoes. She unstrapped the thigh holster holding the palm-sized .22 pistol and the thin knife and sheath taped to the other thigh. An ankle holster from the go-bag was then strapped to her right ankle and filled with a .32 from the gun case. New medical paper tape and some contortions placed the knife on her back between her shoulder blades, with the tip of the five-inch blade stretching below her bra strap. When the T-shirt with SBI POLICE in big letters on the back and the agency logo on the front was in place, the top of the hilt was two inches below the collar. A pair of jeans completed the ensemble, along with a pair of cross-trainers. She glanced at herself in the mirror to make sure everything was in place and thought that you can take the girl out of Texas, but you can't take the Texas out of the girl.

She repacked the cases, went up to her office to check out at the secretary's desk, then headed back to the car. It was about a two-hour drive from Raleigh down I-40, past Wilmington, to all the beaches. There were dozens of little beach towns all up and down the Carolina coast, most out on barrier islands, and Carolina Beach was one of them. Once off the interstate and onto State 421, she pulled into a QT to fill the car and empty her bladder. She wanted to be ready for anything, including a long boat ride.

She was using her GPS to navigate, but she saw the First Baptist Church, with its long white steps leading up to the sanctuary that the Director had mentioned just before she took the first left turn. The second left put her in a small parking lot next to a lot of docks. Many of them were empty, probably with the boats out at sea, but enough were in port to tell her they were mainly charter boats for tourists fishing by the day, some tour boats, and a couple of party boats. Not a center of commercial fishing, she concluded.

She pulled into a parking space, put the sign on her dashboard identifying her car as being on official police business, and went around to the trunk. She decided she didn't want anyone questioning who she was or that she was serious, so she pulled her shoulder holster from her go-bag and her state-issued Glock from the gun case and covered them up with the state-issued white SBI jacket that left no doubt that she was SBI-Police. Tossing one strap of her backpack over a shoulder, she locked and hid the gun case, then locked the trunk and car.

Looking around, she saw the little booth with the POLICE sign on top right next to the city-owned section of the docks. It was barely bigger than a toll booth, but there was a speedboat labeled Carolina Beach Police in the water just in front of it. She walked over and pulled open the door. Inside was a man with his feet propped up on the counter, leaning back in his chair, watching an Atlanta Braves game rebroadcast on his tablet computer.

"I'm looking for Detective Butts."

She then waited for "the look." She knew most women got the once-over for their curves. She had enough curves to not be mistaken for a man, but it was her height that took them a second to adjust too. She was six feet, one inch in her stocking feet. With the cross-trainers she had on, she was closer to six-three. She never wore spike heels, but she had a pair of stack heels at home for formal occasions that lifted her up to six-five. That took the men a little time to get over.

In addition, she was not some willowy model. She was what her mother delicately called "big-boned." Ranch work on the family spread in West Texas had built plenty of muscle on those big bones and playing basketball in high school and college had led to the habit of lifting weights and running several miles a week. That had gotten her high school team to a division title her senior year with her as the leading player, but college had been a different story. Even going to a little university in Texas, she had ended up as the backup center all four years. It turned out she had a lot more slow-twitch muscle than fast-twitch, so she sat on the bench behind a five-eleven girl who could run the floor with the guards, grab rebounds off the rim, and block more shots than opposing centers were used to. Sara had played when the score got one-sided, one way or another, and when the fast-twitch starter got winded, which happened often enough, that being one of the problems with all that fast-twitch muscle. But basketball past college was destined to be a recreation for Sara. She still played when she could get into an all-women's game, but so many of the recreation leagues these days were co-ed. She had learned that putting on a double move and hitting a hook shot over some guy was no way to make friends among the masculine sex.

"I'm Butts."

Whatever Detective Butts's first impression of her was, he was smart enough to hide it. He was in his forties, just a touch of gray hair, but still looked in good shape.

"Special Agent FitzGerald. You called the SBI."

"My chief did."

"So, what's the story?"

"It will be a lot easier to explain on the scene. Hey, George, SBI is here. Let's go."

Detective Butts was in plain clothes which, in his case, meant tan Docker pants, a green knit shirt, and sneakers. The other officer who appeared, evidently named George, was in uniform, which for beach duty meant a blue, short-sleeve shirt with the appropriate patches, matching Bermuda shorts, deck shoes, and a standard weapons belt. He went straight to the boat while Butts locked up the booth. Once they were in the boat, George tossed them life jackets: Sara slipped hers on over her backpack. George cast off and started the twin Evinrudes that made the boat fast and conversation nearly impossible.

They started up the channel slowly, leaving the commercial docks with the charter fishing boats and passing seemingly endless little docks behind the houses that lined both sides of the channel. Here, the boats ranged from barely more than rowboats with an outboard on the back to boats big enough to have a small cabin below deck. On the starboard side, she could see that there was a row of houses along the water, then a road, then a double row of houses, another road, another row of houses, and nothing beyond, so she figured the ocean must be past the four-deep houses.

As the houses started to thin out, they came to a fork in the channel. It didn't take much guess work to figure out that the left fork led to the Cape Fear River, which led inland to Wilmington. But they took the right fork. On the right, the houses thinned to two rows, then ended entirely, probably along with the road itself. The left side was a marsh. There was a hard turn to starboard, into the channel, and they were quickly out on the open ocean. Here, they turned south, running parallel to the beach. They passed several rows of pilings, looking like telephone poles sticking up out of the water. Sara recognized immediately what they were; the supports of beach houses that elevated the houses several feet. This was common in houses built right on the beach. But the beach seemed to have moved about fifty yards back, and the houses disappeared except for the pilings. Then she saw an exception.

Up ahead was what looked like a giant tuna can on stilts. It was round, big enough to be a house, but steel. There was a floating dock on the water and steps leading up to the house. Another boat was tied to the floating dock, but George expertly guided their boat up to the end of the dock, tied it off, and cut the engines.

"OK, Butts, talk to me."

"It's a hurricane-proof house. Steel walls, aerodynamic shape, no corners or overhangs to catch the wind. Steel shutters on all the windows. Guaranteed to survive winds up to 150 miles an hour. It used to be on the beach, but a couple of years ago we had to dredge the channel. This is a barrier island, so it moves a little each year anyway, but the dredging did something to the currents. Toss in a couple of hurricanes, and the beach is now over there. All the other houses are gone. Had to build a breakwater just down the beach to slow the erosion."

"Fascinating. And we are here why?"

"About nine o'clock this morning, we got a call from a Margaret Anderson, an administrative assistant at Meditrack Software in Raleigh. Their CEO, Richard Davidson, who always gets into the office by eight o'clock, hadn't shown up and wasn't answering his cell phone. One of their techies pinged his cell and it showed he was here. This used to be the model the house company showed potential customers, but when the beach eroded, they built another one further down. Evidently, Davidson owns this house. They asked us to come check on him, thinking he might be sick or hurt or something. George here and another uniform hopped in the boat and came out here. No response, and the place was locked up tight. That would have been the end of it since we didn't have a warrant, but there was that distinctive odor—if you know what I mean. Gave us cause. They looked for a spare key, but nothing. Steel shutters locked from the inside. Steel door in a steel door frame. Really good deadbolt lock. They called back to the station, and I came out with a locksmith. He looked at the lock and just reached for his drill. Drilled out the lock, but door still wouldn't open. Locksmith had to go back for an acetylene torch. Turns out, there was a steel bar on the inside, rotating down into a bracket to hold the door closed no matter what. Had to burn through part of the door and then that steel bar. When we finally got in, this is what we found."

He handed her his tablet showing a picture of a man sprawled in an armchair with lots and lots of bullet holes in him. He wore a Hawaiian-style shirt in garish red and purple, white running shorts, and no shoes. He looked to be about six feet tall, very thin, with brown hair that was swept straight back and fell just below his ears. Sara swiped through the other crime scene pictures. All showed basically the same thing, a dead man and no other disturbance.

"I called the Chief, he called the county coroner and then asked Wilmington to lend us their CSI team. CSIs are still inside. Laptop computer and cell phone were on the coffee table. I checked the vic's dresser, found a wallet with an ID of Richard Davidson, two debit cards, three credit cards, and sixty-five dollars cash. His keys were there too, including what the locksmith said was the key to the deadbolt. But no guns, no shell casings, nothing else seemed out of order. Just a dead guy in the chair. The keys made me wonder how the shooters got out since I didn't see any way to put the door bar in place from outside. So, I checked all the windows. All locked, all the shutters closed and locked from the inside, either with a sliding bolt or a smaller version of the bar like is on the door. That's when I called the

Chief and he called SBI. Hell, I been on the force twenty years, nothing like this. I get B&Es, car thefts, bar fights, tourist stuff; nothing like this."

"OK. Is the body still inside?"

"Naw, Coroner took it away about an hour ago. Preliminary ruling was death by gunshot. Big surprise. Probably about twenty-four hours earlier, say Sunday morning, though that's just a guess right now."

"You said 'shooters' like there was more than one."

"Look close at the pictures. Big wounds and little ones. Most likely a .45 and a .22, though you really can't tell caliber from wound size for sure, but one big gun and one small one, bullets entering at slightly different angles, big gun on the guy's left, little gun on his right, like there were two people sitting on that sofa across from the armchair who just stood up and started shooting across the coffee table. Didn't miss either. Coroner counted nine big and seven small wounds."

"They both emptied their guns."

"Looks that way."

"Then took the time to police their brass, wipe up any prints, lock the house up, and disappear without leaving any trace."

"Assuming they used automatics and not revolvers so there were shells to clean up. And probably ran their boat out to sea a ways to deep water before dumping the guns and shells over-board."

"That would be the smart move."

At that point, the two Wilmington CSIs came down the stairs.

"We're done inside. We need to process the victim's boat."

"Go for it."

"Your prints on file for exclusion?"

"Yeah."

"You weren't gloved?" she asked.

"Not at first. Like I said, we weren't expecting anything like this. Once I realized what was going on, I gloved up."

The second CSI added, "We're taking the laptop and phone

back to the lab, otherwise everything is just like we found it. Should have a report in a day or two, maybe."

"Anything you can tell us now?" asked Sara.

"Everything's encrypted and password protected. This guy knew what he was doing when it came to computers."

"Call his office in Raleigh; they may have some passwords."

"Right."

The CSIs climbed into the other boat and started their examination. Butts turned to Sara.

"You ready to go inside, FitzGerald?"

"Just let me glove up. In case the CSIs have to come back."

She slipped off the life preserver, slipped one arm out of the backpack strap, and swung it around so she could pull a couple of latex gloves out of an outside pocket. That's one of the reasons she carried a backpack, lots of pockets. Even two extra pockets, one inside and one outside, that she had added where they were not obvious. She liked to carry a little more than a wallet, cell phone, and lipstick.

Butts also pulled out a set of latex gloves from a pocket and slipped them on, then led her up the steps to the little porch outside the door. The locksmith had bolted on a place to put a padlock, but it hung open through one ring. Sara stopped on the porch to examine the shutter covering the window next to the door. Open, the shutters would have rested against the steel wall, but closed they fit into the niche of the window, creating a smooth surface for the wind to flow over.

The door was a mess, burn marks around where the deadbolt had been and along the side next to the frame. Inside, all was still neat and clean, if you ignored the fingerprint powder. She walked into the living room: the bloodstained chair, sofa, and coffee table just as in the pictures. Big screen TV on one wall, not much else.

"How did he get electricity?"

"Solar panels on roof. Also, a cistern, solar water heater, and a satellite TV dish. Those are designed to break off and fly away without damaging the roof if the wind gets really bad."

"OK. You seem to know a lot about these houses."

"The sales office is in town. Brochures are all over the hotels."

"Ah."

Sara continued into the bedroom. There was a queen-size bed, but the covers seemed to be rumpled on only one side. Closet held some shirts and shorts, but the victim seemed to have been living out of a small, hard-shell suitcase plopped on a luggage rack. Dresser drawers had a few changes of underwear and socks, but not enough for a week. The other bedroom had bunkbeds and a layer of dust over everything. Bathroom revealed the usual soap and shampoo, bottle of Tylenol, sunscreen, toothpaste and brush, electric razor. Moving into the kitchen, Sara opened the dishwasher: two cereal bowls, two plates, two spoons, two knives, two coffee cups. A partly used loaf of wheat bread was on the counter next to a jar of Jif smooth peanut butter. Cabinet held a box of Cheerios and a box of K-Cups of mountain roast coffee. Refrigerator contained a milk carton and two cans of Coke left from a six-pack.

"This guy was not following a recommended diet."

"He could have gone into a restaurant for meals," said Butts.

"Maybe."

Now Sara retraced her steps through all the rooms, carefully looking at every window and shutter. When she got back to the window beside the door, she pressed in on the side spring locks and lifted the bottom frame. This window had the shutter with the swing bar that fit into a bracket on the other shutter. She lifted the bar and opened the shutters. She then closed them again, letting the bar fall into place. She closed the window and heard the window locks spring into place when it got to the bottom. Then she went back outside and looked all over the porch. She went down the steps and looked at the porch and steps from the bottom. She got down on her knees and crawled around the floating wooden platform feeling the sides with her gloved hands.

"You want us to get a diver and look on the underside?"

"No, if I couldn't reach it from up here, it wouldn't be a practical hiding place."

"For a spare key?"

"Yes."

She sat on the steps.

"Can I secure the scene now?"

"Sure."

Butts went back up the stairs and locked the padlock, then stretched some crime scene tape across the door. He came down the steps, avoiding Sara, and stood on the platform, watching her.

"Well? How did the shooters get out?"

"Not important."

"Not important?"

"I can think of at least three ways to get out and lock up. The windows lock automatically whether they are closed from the inside or the outside. It's the shutters that are the problem. The ones with the sliding bolt you just loop a thread around the little knob once, take the two ends outside so they fit in the crack between shutter halves, close the shutters from outside, pull both ends of the thread until the bolt drops into place, then pull one end of the thread so it slides right out. You might be able to do the same thing with a strong magnet, but I'd have to try it to be sure. But I like coming out the window over the porch so I have someplace outside to stand. You could either pull the same kind of trick with a thread around the bar you use to lower it into place or use a magnet or maybe jam some ice cubes under the bar so that when they melted the bar fell into place. Doesn't really matter how they got out except it tells us they were smart enough to think of something. What I want to know is how they got in and why they locked up when they left."

"I don't get it."

"What's the point of locking up? Was anybody else coming out here? Did they need to delay the body being found for some reason? Or did they just want to try to make the police look dumb? And if so, what have they got against the police? Dumping the guns makes sense, but why not just jump in whatever got you out here and get away as quickly as possible? Why lock up?"

"OK. I think I see your point. Why are you worried about how they got in?"

"The window by the door lets you see who is on the porch. Why did he open the door and let them in? Not a lot of Jehovah's Witnesses or other casual visitors knocking on this door. He probably knew them. If it was somebody he thought was out to get him, why not just leave the door closed and tell them to go to hell? You'd need some kind of military weapon to get in through all that steel. And I think we would have noticed that."

"No kidding."

"Most likely scenario. Not conclusive, but most likely. He drove down from Raleigh Friday night, intending to just stay the weekend. He ate dinner on the road or in town, picked up a few groceries, parked next to wherever his boat was docked, and came out here."

"We're already looking for his car."

"Check his office. Probably has LoJack or something. I suppose it's possible somebody was already in there when he got here, but that still doesn't explain how they got in or why there is only one side of the bed used and only enough plates and bowls for one person for a day and a breakfast. Again, most likely he was here alone all day Saturday and until Sunday morning. Ate Cheerios for breakfast both days, peanut butter sandwiches for lunch and supper Saturday. Coffee for two breakfasts, Coke for lunch and supper. Sunday morning, probably around ten or eleven, two people he knows come out here on a boat or something, pull right up to the dock, knock on the door, he looks out the window to see who it is, and he lets them in. He sits in the armchair, they sit on the sofa. For some reason they all stand up, the two on the sofa pull guns and empty them into him. He falls back into the armchair and dies very quickly. They pick up the shell casings, try to wipe off any fingerprints, lock the place down, and motor away in their boat, or paddle off on their paddle boards, or row off in their sea kayaks, or whatever. Unless they had the spare key. If the bar wasn't in place, they could have let themselves in if they arrived quietly. But I don't know if they could count on the bar being open. But either way, these were probably people he knew who he didn't think were there to kill him."

"OK."

"So, we need to get back to shore and start finding out more about this guy. You check on next of kin?"

"Office in Raleigh says parents dead. Gave me contact info for brother in Phoenix and sister in Yuma, out in Arizona. I called them while I was waiting for you. They both said they would fly to Raleigh as soon as possible. May be in the air by now. You CSIs about done?"

"We're finished."

"George, you take the vic's boat back to the dock, get it trailered into the impound lot. I'll drive the rest of us back in our boat."

"Right."

Again, there was no attempt at conversation over the sound of the motors. Once back at the dock, the CSIs packed up and left, leaving FitzGerald looking at Butts.

"You know anything about Richard Davidson?"

"Not really. I think he used to come here in the summers when he was a kid. His parents ran some candy shops on the boardwalk or something. He never went to school here, far as I know. Supposedly hit it big in computer software. May have some connection to the hurricane house company."

"You said the sales office was here in town."

"Yeah. Guy named Harry Stiles. Has an office in the Tucker Real Estate building."

"Let's start there."

"It's just a block away. You OK with walking?"

"Sure. You know this Harry Stiles?"

"To say hello to. You take out the tourists and the summer-only folks, and this is a really small town."

So, they walked past the back of Sharkie's Burgers and Brews, crossed the street onto Myrtle Avenue for a winding block, then across Harper, and there it was. Tucker Real Estate was in big letters and, as an afterthought, Hurricane-Proof Houses, Inc., in much smaller letters. Butts held the door open for her, and they walked up to a reception counter. The nameplate on the counter said Nancy Tucker, which was probably the lady behind the counter.

"Hey, Nancy, is Harry still here?"

"Yeah, sure, Doug. He get another parking ticket?"

"Naw, we just need to talk to him."

Nancy proceeded to yell down the hall. "Hey, Harry, the police are here to arrest you."

That got three men to pop out of their offices and look toward the counter. Butts started down the hall and Sara followed. He greeted the first two but kept on walking.

"Tom. Elton."

At the end of the hall, Butts stopped in front of the third man. He looked like a salesman, dark blue suit and tie, only with the tie loose and the coat hung on the back of his desk chair. Probably late twenties. Black hair slicked back, handsome but a little too artificial to be taken seriously.

"Harry, you got a few minutes?"

"Sure, Doug. What's up?"

"This is Special Agent FitzGerald from the State Bureau of Investigation. We just need to ask you a few questions."

"Sure. Just let me grab another chair."

Harry ducked across the hall into an empty office and brought back a chair. His little office barely had room for his desk and one visitor's chair, let alone two, but he managed to get it in. Harry went to sit behind his desk, and Sara closed the door that he had left open. Butts started the conversation.

"You heard anything about what happened today?"

"No, what?"

"We found Richard Davidson shot to death up in the old model hurricane house."

"Oh shit. You're kidding."

"Afraid not."

"Damn."

"What was he doing up there?"

"He owns it. Hell, he owns the company. I'm just the sales force. When we couldn't use it as a model anymore, he started using it as a weekend getaway."

"You know why he was there this weekend?"

"No idea. He comes and goes. I think he goes up there to work on his software stuff, you know, when he needs to concentrate or something. I never see him."

Sara took over the questioning.

"He never comes by this office?"

"We do all our business by email. Accountant comes by once a year to check the books. Otherwise, I'm on my own. Only time I ever met him was when I was interviewed and again when I was hired. As long as I make a sale once in a while, I almost never even hear from him."

"Mr. Stiles, do you know anything about a spare key to that house?"

"Sure, I've got it right here."

Harry took a key out of his pocket and unlocked a drawer in his desk, took out a metal lockbox, unlocked that with another key on his ring, and sorted through a group of keys until he found the one he was looking for.

"When we stopped using that house as a model, he had me send him one key, but left the other with me. I go out and check it after a hurricane, that kind of thing."

"Why don't you give that key to Detective Butts. It's not much good anymore anyway."

"We had to break the lock to get in. Wish we'd known you had a key."

"Mr. Stiles, is there any possibility that key could have been taken out of this office during the weekend? Or a duplicate made?"

"No way. It's locked up here, and I have the desk and lockbox keys in my pocket all the time. And nobody gets in this building without creating a stir. Hell, the Tuckers have the keys and security codes to half the houses on the waterfront in their offices. They have locks and security systems and video monitors like you wouldn't believe."

"Why so many keys?"

"They not only help people buy and sell houses, they act as rental agents. Lots of people in the expensive beach houses only come down here a few weeks a year. Rest of the time they rent them out by the week to help cover the mortgage and flood insurance. Tuckers act as their agents, giving the keys and security codes to the renters, checking the houses at the end of each week, dealing with any repairs, that kind of thing. In exchange for a cut of the rent, of course."

"Of course."

"Tell me about Mr. Davidson."

"Well, like I said, I hardly knew him. It was all business with him."

"So, why this business?"

"Well, the story we tell the clients is that when he was a kid, his parents were killed by a hurricane, so when he got older, he hired some engineers to design a hurricane-proof house and he was now dedicated to helping people live safely on the beach."

"And how much of that is true?"

"All of it, as far as it goes. He never lived here year-round, but his parents were schoolteachers up in Raleigh who came down during the summer to run some of the refreshment stands on the boardwalk. He would work ten- to twelve-hour days along with his brother and sister selling snow cones and cotton candy and stuff. His parents had started with just one little stand and eventually owned seven. You know, Doug, the ones Milt Roberts operates now. Your daughter worked at one last summer."

"Yeah."

"Anyway, they had a cheap little cottage up on Sixth, over

near the park, nowhere near the beach, and tried to ride out Fernando, what, eight, ten years ago."

"I remember that one. I was still in uniform, and cops and fire department had to ride it out upstairs in the Baptist church. It got bigger right at the last minute. Power was out for two weeks; several people were killed, and others hurt. I was glad I had sent Emily and the kids to Fayetteville."

"Well, Richard Davidson wasn't exactly a kid at the time. He had just finished college. But his parents crammed the three almost-grown children into a big cast iron bathtub when the storm got bad. Then the roof blew off and a wall came crashing down on them. The three in the tub survived with bruises and scrapes, but the parents were killed. So, he really does have an emotional reason to want to sell hurricane-proof houses. When he got a little ahead financially from the software company, he bought the rights to the design from a couple of Georgia Tech engineering students who did it for a senior project. He got a company that builds metal warehouses to build the first model, took a bunch of pictures, and put up a website. Hired me to respond to all the email queries, keep the website up to date, and show the model to anybody that wanted to see it."

"And you sell a lot of these?"

"Well, we'll build them anywhere in the country, not just here. The buyer has to provide their own lot. Basically, we sell the rights to the design and subcontract with the same construction company to build the house, but it's all wrapped up in one contract for the buyer."

"I'm curious, Mr. Stiles, was Mr. Richardson making a lot of money from this company?"

"Well, since I guess I'm going to be out of a job soon, I can lay it out for you. Houses sell for $500,000, with any upgrades basically at cost. We pay the contractor $400,000 plus whatever the upgrades cost. He can usually build one for around $350,000, so he's making $50,000, plus or minus. Of our $100,000, I get 10 percent, plus enough to cover the rent for this office, web advertising costs, phone, and utilities, etc. Web advertising isn't as cheap as it used to be, especially the narrowly targeted kind we do, but we probably cleared $50,000 a house, which went into his bank account. And I sold twelve houses last year, which was my best year so far. You do the math."

"He wasn't losing money."

"Well, remember, he was on the hook for construction cost of the first model, then had to turn around and pay for the second model to be built, plus the cost of two beachfront lots, plus whatever he paid the guys from Georgia Tech. And there is no insurance for the ocean swallowing the beach from under your house. Nor for hurricane damage if your house isn't damaged, even if you can't get to it anymore. So, he was heavily invested in startup costs. I think he may have been about to break even, but I don't know. All I know is that I was doing pretty well, considering I barely finished high school. Now I don't know what I'll do."

"Don't quit yet, Mr. Stiles; somebody is going to inherit, and they may want to keep riding this horse."

"I sure hope so. He had his finger in a lot of pies though, so you never know."

"What else?"

"Well, the software company was making even more money, I think. And he was getting some every year from the lease on the candy stands."

"Milt doesn't own those?" asked Butts.

"No, he leases by the year. Had them for a long time now, but Davidson still is the owner."

"Mr. Stiles, you understand I have to ask this question, but where were you Sunday morning?"

"Well, I got to church a little after nine. I teach Sunday School at the Methodist church, and I needed to set up for my middle school class. Then I sang in the choir at the worship service. Took the wife to the Shuckin' Shack for lunch. We got home maybe two o'clock. You can ask the pastor, the choir director, ten middle school kids, and about one hundred people in the congregation."

"I may ask Detective Butts to check with a couple of those, but that sounds like a pretty good alibi to me. Thank you for your time, Mr. Stiles. Here's my card if you think of anything else you think I might want to know."

"Yeah, thanks, Harry."

"Who the hell would shoot Davidson, Doug? Hardly anyone here ever even saw him."

"That's what we'd like to know, Harry."

They exited the office and went back down the hall, thanking the Tuckers, who appeared to be waiting on them to leave before closing up, leaving it to Harry to fill them in. Once back out on the street, they stood under a little tree and conferred.

"Well, you can eliminate Harry from the list of suspects; airtight alibi and no motive."

"I was more interested in what he told us about Davidson. What do you know about this Milt Roberts?"

"Major bigwig in town. Owns several beachwear shops, souvenir shops. I thought he owned the food stands too, but I guess I was wrong about that. Let's see, it's suppertime, so he's probably right next door at Pop's Diner, if my guess is right."

"You know him?"

"We're both Deacons at the Baptist church. Like I said, this is really just a small town with lots of visitors. He's a widower who doesn't like his own cooking. He has a regular rotation through the restaurants, and I think today is Pop's Diner."

"Let's give it a shot."

They walked around the corner and down to the next building. Butts opened the door for her again, then looked around.

"That's him, corner booth in the back."

They walked past the other tables and booths to where a man in a white dress shirt, no tie, was cutting into a steak. He was probably early sixties, gray flat-top haircut, with the puffy jowls and stomach of a man who ate too many meals in diners.

"Move over, Milt, you got company."

"Doug, good to see you."

Milt slid over in the booth to make room for Butts, giving Sara the entire seat on the other side.

"Missed you in church on Sunday."

"Was up half the night looking for a missing kid. Fifteen-year-old girl snuck out on mommy and daddy with a fake ID and a credit card to see what life was like at the Irish Bar."

"She OK?"

"Yeah, once she gets over the hangover. But I just could not crawl out of bed the next morning."

"And who is your official-looking friend here?"

"Special Agent FitzGerald, this is Milt Roberts. He owns about half the town but likes to pretend he's just some old man living on social security."

At that point, a waitress appeared and asked to take their orders. Sara hadn't eaten anything since breakfast but knew this was not the time or the place.

"Just coffee for me."

"Same for me."

"Well, welcome to Carolina Beach, Miss FitzGerald. Business or pleasure?"

It was Butts who answered.

"Did you hear about Richard Davidson, Milt?"

"No, what?"

"He was killed yesterday out at that old model hurricane house. We didn't find the body until today."

"Well, that's not good news. Gonna cause me some headaches, anyway. What happened?"

"That's what we're trying to figure out. You did business with him?"

"Leased some of the refreshment stands on the boardwalk from him."

"I thought you owned all your businesses."

"All the beach shops, not the little candy stands. His parents owned those. After they died, I tried to buy them, but no deal. He would lease them to me by the year, but that was all. I got a good price though. Every year he would send me a lease in the mail, same deal every time, not even increases for inflation. I would sign and send it back, then transfer the funds."

Sara took over the questioning.

"So, you never met with him?"

"Just the first time, when we cut the original deal. Anything else was handled by email or snail mail. Not that there was much to it. I did all the managing, hiring and firing, ordering supplies, repainting each season, that kind of thing. He just sat in Raleigh and collected the rent."

"Were you making money?"

"Sure. Not getting rich, but it was worthwhile. Lot of hassle dealing with all the teenagers that have to be hired and trained every summer, checking on them every so often to see which ones were causing trouble. Not your daughter, Doug. I never had to worry about her. But social security doesn't pay enough to live on, so I have to find a way to make do. How is your daughter doing up at that prep school in New England, by the way?"

"She's fine. Glad the winter is over."

"I bet. Must be costing an arm and a leg though."

"Well, you know, you do what you can for your kids."

At that point, the coffee arrived. Sara noticed that Milt was cutting his steak with his left hand, forcing Butts to turn his cup around and hold it left-handed to avoid any clashing elbows. She wondered if the angle of the shots could tell her if either of the shooters was left-handed. As she took her first sip, Milt swallowed a bite of steak and picked up the conversation.

"My lease is set for this year, till December, but do you know if he left a will? I don't want to think about having to renegotiate this with some executor if everything is tied up in probate. Price is probably going to go up just dealing with some relative."

"We're in the early days, Mr. Roberts. Did you know his family?"

"Parents were schoolteachers, just came down for the summer

to run the stands. Three kids, Richard the oldest by about four years. Another son and daughter. They worked the candy stands with their parents. I guess it wasn't much of a vacation for them. None of them ever really became part of the community. They tried to ride out Hurricane Fernando eight years ago. Lesson for you, Miss FitzGerald; you see a hurricane coming, get off these islands. Parents were killed, kids banged up a little, not to mention whatever emotional damage comes with watching a wall fall on your mother and father and not being able to do anything about it."

"I'll keep that in mind. Anything else you can tell me about Richard Davidson?"

"I think he went to Duke, but I don't know in what. Had just graduated the spring before Fernando. Not really a social guy. Smart, but not so good with people, you know. That's about it."

"OK, thank you. Here's my card in case you think of anything else that might help. Or you can call Detective Butts."

"Doug, you let me know what you find. OK?"

"Sure, Milt."

Sara pulled her wallet out of her backpack to get some ones for the coffee.

"I'll get that."

"Thank you, Mr. Roberts, but regulations forbid."

She laid three dollars on the table. Doug also dug out his wallet and put a couple of ones on the table.

"See you later, Milt."

"Yeah. You two take care."

They exited the diner and started walking slowly back to the docks.

"The brother and sister are flying into Raleigh, right?" asked Sara.

"They said they would go to the old home place where Richard was still living."

"Well, I guess the next step is to talk to them and the people at the Meditrack company."

"I can text you the contact info, but this is my case, and I want to be in those interviews."

"Can you meet me at SBI in Raleigh first thing in the morning?"

"I can. Nine o'clock early enough?"

"That works. Well, I'm going to head back tonight. The sun is pretty far down, and I don't like to drive in the dark more than I have to."

"Understandable."

They got back to her car, said their goodbyes, and Sara drove back the way she had come. Once she was back on the interstate, she thought about stopping to eat, or at least take off the shoulder holster, but she was afraid a big meal would make her drowsy, so she plowed on. Once back at the parking lot for her one-bedroom apartment in the gated complex, she unloaded the go-bag and the gun case from the trunk and carried them back into her apartment. Locking her apartment door behind her, she thought how little security the gate at the entrance to the complex, the peephole on her door, and the basic deadbolt really provided. Richard Davidson had been fifty yards from land, with a steel house, and a window to see who was at the door, and he was dead. Not a reassuring thought.

She locked the gun case and the guns and weapons she had on her in her gun safe and plopped the suitcase on the sofa to deal with later. She checked her text and email on her phone to see if she had anything from the office. There was only a series of texts from Butts with the contact information for the brother and sister and the contact at Meditrack. She did not even consider wasting time on Facebook or Twitter. She stripped off her clothes, used the toilet and the shower, brushed her teeth, and crawled into bed, hungry but too tired to do anything about it. Puzzles and bloody pictures kept worming into her mind, a man nobody seemed to deal with except by email who somebody had gone offshore to visit, two types of guns and massive overkill, all kinds of businesses and money entangled. She couldn't seem to relax enough to get to sleep.

Finally, she reached between her legs and distracted herself until she tensed, then relaxed, and she was able to roll over and drift off to dreamland.

Tuesday

The alarm rang at six o'clock. Sara rolled out of bed, hit the head, and strapped on a sports bra and panties, then running shorts and a T-shirt. She took the stairs down to the apartment complex exercise room, ran a couple of miles on the treadmill, and did a brief upper-body workout on the weight machines. Back in her apartment, she stripped and stepped into the shower, taking the time to wash her shoulder-length brown hair. After drying off, she put her hair in a ponytail and applied some basic makeup.

Sliding on the flannel nightgown she used as a bathrobe, she decided after fasting most of the day before to have a hearty breakfast. She dropped a couple of strips of bacon in a frying pan, put a couple of slices of wheat bread in a toaster, and turned on CNN to see if the world was still there. Buttering the first couple of pieces of toast, she put two more in the toaster, took the cooked bacon out of the pan, then scrambled a couple of eggs in the drippings. Once the eggs and second round of toast were done, she sat down to eat. Switching to the local news, she heard no rain was forecast for the day, turned off the TV, and washed her dishes.

Next, she turned to her go bag. Opening the suitcase, she took out the dress she had worn part of the day before and tossed it in the laundry basket. She replaced the underwear, jeans, and T-shirt with fresh ones, but put the cross-trainers back in after brushing off any sand. Deciding to be a little more business-dressy today, she pulled a white shirt, blue skirt, and matching jacket out of her closet. Shedding her nightgown, she put on underwear, strapped on the thigh holster and knife, and got the .22 from the gun case. She then repacked the other guns in the gun case and holsters in the go-bag. Finally, she pulled on the blouse, skirt, and jacket, checked herself in the mirror, grabbed the go-bag and gun case, and headed for the office.

Promptly at nine o'clock, her desk phone rang.

"Agent FitzGerald."

"This is the security desk in the lobby. A Detective Butts is here to see you."

"Tell him I'll be right down."

She saved her files, logged off, grabbed her backpack from the drawer, signaled her exit to the secretary, and headed for the stairs. Butts was standing in the lobby waiting.

"Good morning."

"Thank you for being on time. We have a nine-thirty appointment to see the brother, Dwight. We can take my car."

She led him out of the lobby into the agent's parking garage, indicated which was her car, unlocked it remotely, and climbed into the driver's seat. Once on the road, she continued briefing Butts.

"He's at what he called the old home place, where they grew up. Evidently, Richard still lived there. His sister, Cynthia, is there too, but she was on a later flight and may not be up yet."

"OK."

"Listen, Butts, I know you think this is your case, but you're out of your jurisdiction. Let me take the lead on this, OK?"

"Not a problem."

"Good."

They soon pulled up in front of a small brick house that looked like it was built in the 1950s, when houses still came with front and back yards. There were trees that towered over the house, having been there at least as long as the house. It was a middle-class neighborhood that had somehow endured all the urban renewal and swings in property values, a shaded two-lane street with little traffic and neighbors who might actually know each other.

They rang the doorbell and flashed their badges when a man in his late twenties answered the door. He was wearing what would become a brown suit once the coat and tie were added, about five feet, ten inches, with an already receding hairline and short brown hair.

"Mr. Dwight Davidson?"

"Yes."

"I'm Special Agent FitzGerald with the North Carolina State Bureau of Investigation. This is Detective Butts from the Carolina Beach Police Department."

"Yes, come in."

He led them into the living room, which was neat and clean, but looked like it still had the same furniture as when Dwight Davidson was a little boy, sturdy and well-built but of a different era. He indicated they should sit on the sofa, while he took a large chair placed at a ninety-degree angle, with a coffee table in the center.

"Thank you for seeing us so early, Mr. Davidson. We're sorry for your loss."

"Thank you. Could you tell me any more about what happened? All I got on the call with Detective Butts yesterday was that my brother had been shot and killed Sunday morning at the hurricane house on the beach."

"That's still basically all we know, Mr. Davidson. It wasn't a robbery as far as we can tell, but it's still early in the investigation. We are hoping you or your sister could tell us if there was any reason someone would want to kill your brother."

"My sister is upstairs asleep. Coming from Yuma, she had to take a much later flight and didn't get in until very late. As for who would want to kill my brother, once you eliminate me and my sister, I have no idea."

"And why would you and your sister want to kill Richard?"

"Well, for the record, if Richard was killed on Sunday morning, in Arizona that would be three hours earlier since Arizona doesn't go on Daylight Savings Time. I was sound asleep at home, but was seen by dozens of people at Camelback Church around nine-thirty, and let me tell you, there is no way to get from Phoenix to Raleigh in an hour and a half, or even two and a half. As for my sister, she was finishing up her shift at the Yuma Area Hospital, so you can scratch her off the list of suspects too."

"I'm more interested in why anybody would want to kill your brother."

"OK. Let's see. How much time have you got?"

"As long as it takes."

"OK. This makes more sense from the beginning, even before the beginning. Our parents were orphans. Grew up in a series of orphanages and foster homes, he in North Carolina; she in South Carolina. Never quite got adopted. When they turned eighteen, they were cut loose, no state support, so they joined the army. But they had managed to graduate high school, and were not unmotivated, so in the army they started taking college courses. The army helps pay for that, you know, correspondence courses back then, online stuff now."

"Yes."

"So, when their tours of duty were up, they had some good grades and college credits, plus the GI Bill. They managed to get into UNC. That's where they met, at some function for veterans. They discovered they had a lot in common, one thing led to another, and they were married at the courthouse the week after they graduated. They both had teaching jobs lined up for the Fall; my father taught high school math. That's probably where Richard got his talent with numbers. My mother taught fifth grade, just before the kids went wild, as she put it.

"Anyway, they didn't have money for a real honeymoon, but they went down to Carolina Beach for a weekend. Walking on the boardwalk, they saw a sign for help wanted at one of the refreshment stands. They didn't have anything lined up before school started, so they asked about the jobs. It didn't pay much, but with both of them working they could rent a real cheap room and keep body and soul together until September rolled around and they went back to Raleigh.

"Anyway, that sort of started it all. They knew they were going to be out of school every summer except for an occasional professional development course, so they leased another one of the refreshment stands for a summer, then bought it. Sold fudge and salt-water taffy my mom made in a little kitchen in the back of the stand. In a couple of years, Richard comes along, but they just bring him with them. Though they did buy this little cottage way off the beach to live in during the summer instead of trying to live in a rental with a little baby.

"My parents didn't exactly have a good parenting model to follow; they just sort of did what made sense to them. Keeping a kid in that little stand twelve hours a day, seven days a week made sense to them. But Richard was smart, very smart, I'll give him that. I came along a little over four years later, and one of my earliest memories is of him operating the cash register and making change.

"By then, they had bought a little hole-in-the-wall place two doors down, barely bigger than a broom closet, that sold snow cones through a window. By the time Richard was twelve, he was running that by himself. They kept buying new spaces; cotton candy, cold drinks, soft-serve ice cream. They would hire high school kids until one of us got old enough to run it ourselves. You may not believe this, but I never actually went in the water on the beach. We would show up the day after school closed, open the booths, and from then on we walked down from the cottage to set up, ran the booth for twelve hours, cleaned up and locked up, then walked home, all five of us, getting in long past dark. Went on that way until the day before school opened, when we locked up for the winter and drove back to Raleigh.

"Then, of course, my parents were busy with school. Anybody who thinks teachers have short days doesn't know what they are talking about. We got fed and dealt the basics, but we pretty much had to raise ourselves. Richard was the responsible one, but he hadn't had much of a childhood. He didn't seem to really understand the idea of "playing" or "fun." Did you go to college, Agent FitzGerald?"

"Yes."

"Well, maybe you met the kind of student who double majored in two totally unrelated, difficult subjects and took the hardest classes just to see how he would do."

"I know people like that."

"Well, for Richard it was premed and computer science. Graduated magna cum laude from Duke, but I don't think he had a date the entire time he was there. Didn't go to football or basketball games, didn't visit the museums, didn't go to plays or concerts. Only thing that got his nose out of a book was running cross-country and long-distance races in track, and I think he only did that because he could pretty much train alone.

"Anyway, I guess you've heard the story of how the summer after he graduated, we were down at the beach, working away as usual. There was a hurricane coming, but it wasn't supposed to be too bad, and my parents wanted to make as much money as possible with Richard enrolled at Duke med school and me accepted into UNC, so they decided to stay open as long as possible, ride out the storm, and open back up as soon as possible."

"We have been told the outline of that, but please, you know details we haven't heard."

"Well, that little cottage was back on Sixth Street, well away from the beach, three feet up on stilts, and had made it through dozens of storms over the years. But that year something went wrong. The storm was worse than forecast. We all crowded into the bathroom, and my father made all three of us cram into the bathtub while he and my mother sat on the edge. It was the middle of the night; the power was out when the roof flew off. Just took off into the air like an airplane. I guess that just took away something that was helping hold up the frame of the house because within seconds the walls were crashing down. I guess we were all screaming because all I remember is screams and bodies pressing down on me. Then the eye passed over us, and we got a few minutes of dead calm. Just long enough to discover that the wall studs had fallen on our parents. To this day I don't know whether they were dead or just badly hurt at that point, but then the storm came back and Richard pushed us back into the bathtub until the wind calmed down a couple of hours later. By then, our parents were dead. We just sat there in the ruins until some firemen came by and discovered us."

"That must have been terrifying."

"We're still trying to get over it. Never will, I guess. But the thing that estranged us from Richard is what happened after that. I was a couple of months short of eighteen; Cynthia was barely sixteen. Richard was twenty-two. My parents' wills made him our guardian. Also made him executor of the wills. I guess our parents didn't have anybody else they trusted. And there was a good bit of money involved. Two life insurance policies through the school district, the house insurance for the cottage at the beach that Richard cashed out instead of rebuilding, and the money our parents had been saving for college tuitions.

"Some things he did I agree with. There wasn't much left on the mortgage on this place, so he paid that off. He leased the refreshment stands to Milt Roberts so we never had to work in those again. Should have just sold them. But instead of going to med school, he decided to start his own software company developing medical records tracking software for doctors and clinics. Poured all that money into office rent and computers and salaries for a few programmers. He insisted I live here to help look after Cynthia instead of going to UNC. I thought he should have been the one to look after her, and I guess technically he did, but he spent more nights working and sleeping in the little office he rented than he did here.

"I ended up having to go to a local junior college for one year because it was too late to get in anywhere else close. I did manage to get into NC State the next year, but I had to commute and live here. Not the college experience I had planned. I will admit, we never went hungry and he paid tuition and fees and books and basics, but not much more. Cynthia ended up not going to her senior prom because he wouldn't spring for a prom gown. Eating out was never an option. Days I couldn't make it home from State for lunch, I had to brown-bag it. He never seemed to understand there was more to life than studying or going to class.

"Not that he wasn't working hard. Every waking hour for him went into building that software. We were an interruption to his concentration. He did pony up for my master's in education, but that was more because he wanted me to stay here for another two years until Cynthia finished her bachelor of nursing degree at State. I didn't even apply for teaching jobs in North Carolina, or the Southeast for that matter. I just wanted to get as far away from him as I could.

"So, I teach high school English in Phoenix, Arizona. When I got that job, Cynthia started applying for nursing jobs in Arizona and got on at a hospital down in Yuma. Neither one of us is getting rich; and we certainly haven't gotten any money from Richard. But I eat out at restaurants, I go to concerts, I even have a serious girlfriend. Cynthia is living a normal life too. No thanks to Richard, even though I think there's plenty of money coming in now. He's probably plowing it into some new project, like the hurricane houses or something else."

"I see."

"So, Agent, while I'm sorry he was killed, neither one of us is especially broken up about it."

"Do you know if Richard had a will?

"I assume so. With all those businesses he would be required to, wouldn't he? I have no idea what's in it. Frankly, I would be surprised if Cynthia and I got much out of it."

"Do you know if he was having problems with any of his businesses or people he worked with? Or if there were any personal friends that may have had some emotional involvement?"

"I haven't spoken to my brother since I moved to Arizona two years ago. I can tell you I would be very surprised if there was anybody with any 'emotional involvement' with him."

"Do you have any questions, Detective Butts?"

"Do you know why he kept the hurricane house after it could no longer be used as a model?"

"No idea. I've never even seen it. I haven't been back to the beach since my parents died."

"That's it for me."

"Well, we thank you for your time, Mr. Davidson. We will probably want to speak to your sister, but that can wait until another time. We will keep you informed as things develop. In the meantime, if you can look through your brother's papers and find out which bank he used and call them and see if he had a safety deposit box, it would be a good idea. That might contain a will. If you find one, please let us know."

"Good idea. I guess we are going to have to plan a funeral later today. Do you know when we can have the body?"

Butts replied, "Since it was a violent death, there will have to be an autopsy. The New Hanover County Medical Examiner's Office will notify whichever funeral home you select when the body is released, and they will notify you. I'm sure it will be at least two or three days. The funeral home will know how to contact them to get a better estimate."

"OK, thank you."

"Here's my card. Call me if anything comes up."

"Thank you."

And they were out the door and back in the car.

"Well, Special Agent, what do you think?"

"I think it's time to talk to the people at Meditrack."

She drove them to the office building and parked in the parking lot, putting her "Police" sign on the dashboard again. It was a standard office building, steel and windows, about ten stories tall. According to the office listing in the lobby, Meditrack occupied the fourth and fifth floors. Taking the elevator up got them to the Meditrack lobby, which was not furnished to handle many visitors. Asking for Margaret Anderson and flashing their badges got them taken immediately back to an office along one wall next to an even bigger office with RICHARD DAVIDSON, PRESIDENT on the door. They were taken into the smaller office, where a woman in her thirties, dressed in a power-red dress, jet-black hair cut in a bob, and no makeup, greeted them.

"I'm Margaret Anderson, Mr. Davidson's Senior Administrative Associate. Please sit down."

Sara closed the office door behind her and took one of the chairs in front of the desk while Butts took the other.

"I'm Special Agent FitzGerald of the North Carolina State Bureau of Investigation. This is Detective Butts from the Carolina Beach Police Department. We need to talk to you about Richard Davidson."

"Yes, of course."

"You were Mr. Davidson's secretary?"

"Well, a little more than that. More like deputy for administration. He developed the software, I handled the business side."

"You've been here several years?"

"Almost since the beginning."

"Can you tell me exactly what the business is, Miss Anderson?"

"We develop and market an electronic medical records software program. Doctors and clinics input patient data and can call it up on a computer or a tablet, real-time, right in the office, or track data over time, do billing, file insurance claims directly, submit required data to the Feds, just about anything related to medical records, without having to keep huge file rooms of patient charts. We get input from doctors in actual practice and keep the software up to date as medical practice changes. It saves medical personnel hours of time, prevents some types of mistakes, and reduces costs, which as you know, is a major issue in medicine these days."

"And Mr. Davidson developed this software program?"

"He's the genius behind all the software, yes. He practically wrote the basic program all by himself, designed the entire system. Hired a few programmers to help build it out, then hired me and a few other non-programmer types to market it and run the business. We're up to almost one hundred employees now, keeping the software up-to-date, marketing it across the country, providing technical support, making sure the rent and paychecks get processed."

"So, you're doing well financially?"

"Business has been on the upswing ever since electronic medical records became legally required. We're not the only shark in the water, but we're holding our own."

"Miss Anderson, you understand there are some questions I have to ask you."

"Yes."

"Did you have a non-business relationship with Mr. Davidson?"

"You mean were we lovers? God, no. Richard was a genius, but he couldn't relate to anything that wasn't in a computer. Almost borderline autistic sometimes. I mean computer engineers tend to have strange personalities to begin with, but Richard was on another level, practically withdrawn. We never even had lunch together."

"Do you know of anyone else that might have had a relationship with him? Women or men?"

"He related to computers; that was about it. I think he was straight, but sex drive was not a motivating factor in his life. At least not in anything having to do with the office. And, like I said, I don't think he had a private life."

"Where were you Sunday morning?"

"In bed in the Grove Park Inn in Ashville, enjoying the morning with a gentleman, if you get my drift. We drove back after lunch at the inn. I'm sure I'm on security cameras in the lobby and restaurant around noon. I can give you a name if I have to, but I'm going to wait on that until it's necessary."

"When did you see Mr. Davidson last?"

"When I left at five o'clock on Friday. He was still in his office."

"Did you know Mr. Davidson was going to the beach this weekend?"

"No."

"Would anybody else here in the office have known that?"

"He never told anybody here where he was going or what he was doing outside the office. But he was always available by cell phone or text, twenty-four seven, wherever he was. At least until Monday morning. When he didn't respond Monday morning, we knew something was wrong."

"Did you know he had a house at Carolina Beach?"

"Yes, or at least we knew he had a place to go somewhere on some beach when he wanted to get away from interruptions. He was working on a new cell phone app to tie into the main program, and probably wanted some quiet. We wouldn't have known exactly where without the tracking program on his phone."

"Is there any reason you know of that someone would have wanted to harm him?"

"I guess I should tell you. It's not public knowledge, so we would appreciate you keeping this quiet. But we were in negotiations to be bought out by one of the software giants. I can't tell you which one. Most of us working here have been paid lower than average salaries in exchange for shares in the company. We would all have made big bucks when the deal went through. Especially those of us who have been here a long time. Without Richard, I don't even know if the whole thing will fall apart or not. The other company seemed as interested in having Richard on their payroll as owning the software. But nobody in this company benefitted from the death of Richard Davidson. Nobody particularly liked him as a person, but nobody hated him for personal reasons either, and he was the goose that was about a lay the golden egg, so his death has messed up our lives, big time. You're barking up the wrong tree here, Miss Fitzgerald."

"I see. That is important information. Thank you for telling us. Do you know if Mr. Davidson had made a will?"

"Believe me, we've been asking that same question. I contacted the lawyer the company keeps on retainer, but he says he didn't prepare one. I have been through all the legal files and other documents Richard kept in his office, but so far I haven't found a will. The bank won't give me access to his safety deposit box, which I guess is legal and proper. I guess I will have to have his brother or sister do that."

"Do you know which bank it might be in?"

"Bank of America, probably the main office downtown would be my guess. He did most of his banking electronically. Bank of America was what he used, but I'm not sure about the branch."

"His brother might want to know that."

"I'll let him know as soon as we finish."

"What other questions should I be asking?"

"God, I don't know. This was a total shock to everybody here. If he had been swindling people or selling bad software or having affairs or something I might have expected something. Strange as he sometimes was, he was a straight arrow and all business."

"Can you give me a copy of his personnel file, please."

"I can email it to you. Everything's electronic here."

"OK, here's my card with my email address."

"And mine, please"

"Certainly, Detective."

"We may wish to speak to you again, or to some of the employees."

"We will provide full cooperation. We want this settled as much as you do."

"Thank you.

And they bid their good-byes and went back to Sara's car.

"FitzGerald, is there any possibility we could go somewhere and talk about this case? Maybe over lunch? My stomach is growling."

"I think that can be arranged."

She took him to Grandson's Buffet. It was a red, barn-like building specializing in all-you-can-eat down-home cooking just off 401, near the SBI offices. There were four buffet bars with everything from East Carolina barbeque to bone-in fish to banana pudding for dessert. After they had filled their plates, they sat at one of the tables near the back, where it was still crowded with the tail end of the lunch rush. She saw he must have been hungry because he moved his iced tea to the left side of the plate so he could grab a gulp without having to put down the fork in his right hand. It was too noisy for conversation at first, but after a few minutes the lunch crowd had thinned out and Butts had dulled the edge of his hunger.

"Did you bring me here because it would be too crowded to talk?"

"You said you were hungry. You like the food?"

"The food is great. I'm sure my hunger will be satisfied. I'm not so sure about my curiosity."

"This is a little too public a place to talk about the case."

"So, tell me about you. You're a little young to be an SBI Special Agent, aren't you?"

"There's no age requirement."

"But experience?"

"Sometimes education can substitute."

"Such as?

"Master's in Criminal Justice from UNC-Charlotte."

"Damn, FitzGerald, it's like pulling teeth to get anything out of you."

"Adjunct instructor for one of the courses there was an SBI Special Agent in Charge in the region. He put in a good word for me."

"Look, I'm just a two-bit detective from a little beach town in North Carolina, but even I know there has to be more to it than that."

"It was one of those rare occasions where it was an advantage to be a woman. They were under a lot of pressure to get some diversity among their agents."

"And?"

"And I had certain skill sets they were looking for."

"Such as?"

"Undergrad degrees in psychology and math. Publications on criminal psychology, research in statistics, especially analysis of large data sets."

"They don't give their data analysts badges and guns."

"You don't give up, do you, Butts."

"I like to know who I'm dealing with. You've been a quiet one. Haven't had time to look you up online."

"The SAC at Charlotte persuaded them to give me a little try-out. I scored one hundred at the gun range, out-drove their driving instructor, beat up the self-defense instructor, and ran the fitness instructor into the ground. That got me into the SBI Academy, where I graduated with the highest ranking. You happy now?"

"That helps. Where did you pick up all those skills?"

"I grew up on a ranch in West Texas. We had lots of coyotes and snakes on the range, so my father taught me to shoot as soon as I could hold a gun. I was driving ATVs and pickups as soon as my feet could reach the pedals, which as you can tell, didn't take very long. I can also ride a horse pretty well, but they didn't ask for that at the Academy. I had two older brothers; one was into mixed martial arts and the other studied karate and judo. I was their punching bag and sparring partner until I started punching back and got better than they were. I played basketball in high school and college; training for that included a lot of weightlifting and running. I don't play much basketball anymore, but I kept up the weightlifting and running."

"Where'd you go to college?"

"Little university in San Antonio. What about you, Butts, what's your story?"

"Trying to change the subject."

"Let's just say I believe in equality."

"Born and raised in Carolina Beach. Was not a stellar student. Went to the New Hanover Police Academy straight out of high school. Police Chief back then was a family friend; gave me the first opening he had. Been on the force ever since, working my way up. Went to UNC-Wilmington part-time, finally got a degree after fifteen years. That helped qualify me for detective."

"Family?"

"Wife, two daughters, and a son, in that order."

"Which daughter is in the prep school?"

"Oldest. Other is going into high school in the fall, boy will be in middle school."

"And you're a deacon at the Baptist church."

"It's a small church. Just about everybody has to do something to keep it going."

"Which is where the police ride out hurricanes."

"It's a brick building; sanctuary is upstairs, probably ten feet above ground. It's back from the beach, on the other side of the highway, unlike the police department, which seems to get flooded even by a little storm. Those of us who have to stay on the island, police and fire, go there so we can handle whatever needs handling as soon as the storm is over. Been that way since before I was born."

"We good now?"

"For the moment. I still want to talk about the case soon."

"I'm going to hit the dessert bar."

That ended the conversation until they were back in the SBI parking lot. Butts didn't get in his car as Sara was dropping him off in the public parking but leaned back against the side of the Corolla.

"OK, before we go running off our separate ways, let's talk about this."

"Well, what do you think?"

"I think we got shit. Everybody has alibis and nobody had a motive."

"Alibis need to be checked out. Still waiting on the autopsy report and the CSI findings."

"Autopsy report will show he died of gunshot wounds; CSI won't find zilch."

"Probably. May get a narrower range for the time of death."

"Not by much. Hour or two maybe. That won't change anything with the alibis."

"We follow procedure."

"OK, OK. I'll ask my wife if Newt was in church Sunday morning and call the pastor at the Methodist church to check on Harry. Can you call Grove Park Inn; they're more likely to give you video than me."

"I'll handle Ashville and the two in Arizona. What I want is more on Richard Davidson. What has he been doing in Carolina Beach besides leasing refreshment stands and working on programming? How much time has he been spending down there? Does he eat out, go to bars, go beach combing? He seems to have kept his private life away from the office, but that doesn't mean he didn't have one. He may have been a strange personality, so maybe he lurked in strange places."

"I'll see what I can dig up, but I'm guessing he was more likely weird online instead of in real life."

"Then maybe the CSI guys can give us something after all."

"OK, OK. You'll call me."

"And you call me."

"Deal."

And she drove off to the agent parking lot as he got in his car for the drive home. Once back in her office, she started making phone calls and doing online research. The Grove Park Inn declined to send any video recordings, but after she emailed them a photo of Margaret Anderson she captured from the Meditrack website, the director of security there was willing to call back and "unofficially" confirm that a person resembling the person in the picture was at the inn on Sunday morning. The hospital in Yuma was more cooperative. The security person there checked their duty logs and called a couple of nurses who had been on duty Sunday morning and affirmed that Cynthia Davidson had worked her shift Sunday morning. The Camelback Bible Church in Phoenix turned out to have half a dozen pastors and hundreds of people at each service, but when one of the pastors asked around the office, he was able to call back and say one of the staff remembered Dwight Davidson being in the 9:30 worship service on Sunday. So all the alibis were checking out.

While waiting for callbacks, Sara went digging on the Internet. The Meditrack website was more a promotional piece about the software, with little more than a picture and a brief blurb about the higher-ups in the firm. She learned more about electronic medical records, but very little about Richard Davidson. Same for the Hurricane-Proof House company; lots about the houses, little about Richard Davidson beyond the origin story of the company, and nothing at all about Harry Stiles. A Google search for Richard Davidson turned up more than was on the company websites, but nothing she didn't already know. For a computer software company founder and owner, he didn't seem to have much of an electronic footprint. Then the Meditrack personnel file for Richard Davidson came in from Margaret Anderson, but that had little more than leave records. He was the owner, got paid a regular salary that was decent for a CEO, but not excessive like so many these days. He never seemed to take a day off. And there were no performance evaluations, evidently since he was the top dog and didn't believe in formal evaluations by those he supervised.

It all seemed useless, but at least there was something, which was more than she could say for Milt Roberts. His beachwear and souvenir shops had websites, but Milt wasn't mentioned, and he didn't seem to have any presence on social media. Harry Stiles did have a Facebook presence, but there didn't seem to be anything unusual except for lots of pictures of sunrises over the beach.

On a whim, Sara searched for Douglas Butts. There was some information, but just the basics of his schools and employment. No contact information, family names, or anything personal. She was not surprised, since a lot of cops had found it safer to keep a low social media profile. On a hunch, she tried the First Baptist Church of Carolina Beach website. That had a list and a little blurb about each deacon. She was not surprised they were all men, since West Texas was full of Southern Baptist churches. All she really learned about Butts was that his wife's name was Emily, his daughters were Eliza and Ester, and his son was Gregory.

Late in the afternoon, she got a text from Butts saying nothing more than, "All alibis check out." She also got the preliminary autopsy report from the New Hanover ME. It was preliminary since the tox screens hadn't come back yet, but the rest was there. Death by three .45 bullets to the heart and two .22 slugs to the brain, plus all the other wounds. No sign of defensive wounds, meaning there hadn't been a struggle. The shots had been close range, less than three feet, but not right against the skin. The angle and placement of the bullet holes indicated the shooters had been right in front of the victim, between two and three feet apart, with the .45 on the victim's left and the .22 on the right. At first, the victim had been standing, but as the shooting continued, he fell backward into the chair. Death would have been nearly instantaneous.

Sara considered that a small mercy, but still wondered what Richard Davidson had been thinking when he saw the two guns pointed at him just before they fired. It was not a question that would ever be answered.

By the time all the calls had been returned, all the web searches completed, and all the reports read, it was almost seven o'clock. Sara went back to her apartment and, after the big meal at Grandson's Buffet, settled for an apple and some unsweet iced tea with a splash of lemonade as her supper. She checked her phone, email, and Facebook, but there was nothing new. She caught a little of the Braves game on TV but decided not to stay up to see who won, turning in a few minutes early.

Wednesday

It was Wednesday. Sara got up and this time did a five-mile run on a jogging trail that was close to her apartment complex, then stopped in the apartment exercise room for a little weight training before going up to shower and change. Breakfast was a couple of protein bars and a glass of grape juice. She went with the ankle holster and a pants suit, blue with a green shirt. Once in the office and having checked her emails, she put in a call to the Wilmington CSIs for a status on their report.

The oral report was that no fingerprints had been found that didn't match the victim or one of the three police and the locksmith who had found the body. No DNA or trace evidence had been found that was expected to be other than the victim. They had gotten some passwords from Meditrack and Dwight Davidson, but the phone log and texts reveled nothing but calls to or from Meditrack for the past three months. The laptop was more of a surprise. The log of Internet sites visited seemed innocent enough, mostly checking news and weather, but the victim had three email addresses on three different email sites. One appeared to be for Meditrack business and was all business, as far as they could tell. The second was for personal use, but that seemed to amount to a couple of emails to Harry Stiles related to the hurricane houses and one each to Dwight Davidson and Cynthia Davidson wishing them a happy birthday on the appropriate days.

It was the third address that was the surprise. It required three-factor authentication. Nobody could provide a password for that one and they hadn't been able to crack it yet. Whatever secrets that address held may be beyond their reach. In addition, there were three text files on the computer that evidently were double-encrypted. There were just named FILE 1, FILE 2, and FILE 3, so they had no idea what was inside except that they were documents. They promised to try a little longer, but they had other cases in their own jurisdiction stacking up. The written report would take another two or three days. Sara asked them to send what they had on all the emails and files to the SBI cyber techs, but she didn't hold out much hope.

She knew that Butts had been copied on the autopsy report but sent him a short email summarizing what she had learned over the phone from the CSIs. The expected call from Butts came in twenty minutes later.

"Thank you for keeping me in the loop."

"Not a problem."

"So, what now?"

"Richard Davidson is still the key. Somebody wanted him dead, but why? Who else was he interacting with?"

"You think he had some kind of secret life?"

"Well, he had something going on he wanted to keep secret, if that third email address and three encrypted files are any indication."

"Pedophile, maybe?"

"Maybe, but no pictures of any kind on his laptop."

"Maybe he had a second computer."

"Possible, I guess."

"Hidden at his house?"

"Possible."

"You want me to come up and help look?"

"Well, we're not about to get a search warrant on something this thin, so we're going to have to work something out with his brother and sister. I also need to check on whether anybody has found a will yet. But I'm still curious about whether Davidson did anything else at the beach besides write code and collect rent. Why don't you work your end a little more, at least until I get something agreed with the siblings? They probably don't want us tossing their ancestral home on short notice."

"OK, sounds good. Let me know."

"Right."

And Sara hung up the phone and stared at the SBI logo on her computer screen for several minutes. Then she called the Davidson residence.

"Hello."

"Mr. Davidson, this is Special Agent FitzGerald."

"Yes."

"I was just checking to see if you had received a call from Margaret Anderson at Meditrack. She said she might have some information that would help you in your search for a will, and I asked her to contact you."

"Yes, she called yesterday afternoon. She thinks if Richard had a safety deposit box it would be at the Bank of America downtown."

"And?"

"Usual bureaucracy. They won't tell us anything unless we have a death certificate, which we can't get until the coroner rules on cause of death. Then we will have to have an officer of the court present to make sure all we take out is the will, since we may not be the executor of the estate, which we won't know until we see the will, etc., etc., etc."

"That sounds very frustrating."

"No kidding. We can't schedule a funeral; we can't even pay Richard's bills should anything come in the mail."

"He probably has some kind of automatic bill pay set up."

"I certainly hope so. By the way, Agent, I hear you have been checking our alibis."

"Just routine procedure, sir. I'm sure you understand."

"Yeah, sure, whatever. It's not earning my sister any brownie points at the hospital, having to have the security staff check her out."

"I'm glad you brought your sister up, sir. I really need to meet with her. Just a formality, but part of the procedure."

"I'm not so sure that's a good idea. This whole experience is hard on her."

"I'm sure it is, sir. But I'm afraid it's required. I can come to your house at her convenience."

"Can't she do this over the phone?"

"I'm afraid not. It has to be face-to-face."

"Let me talk to her. I'll call you back."

"She can reach me at the number on my card."

"I have it."

"Thank you, Mr. Davidson. I'll expect to hear from her soon."

"Right. Goodbye."

The call ended. Sara turned to writing up reports of what she had so far. Ten minutes later, the phone rang.

"Special Agent Fitzgerald."

"This is Cynthia Davidson. I understand you want to talk to me."

"Yes, thank you for calling. Is there a time I could meet with you at Richard's house?"

"I've been trying to go through all Richard's things before I have to go back to Yuma, but I guess I can take a break. Can you be here in half an hour?"

"Traffic permitting, yes."

"See you then."

Sara stayed at her desk long enough to text Butts.

Sister wants to meet NOW.

She then headed to her car. Just as she got there she got a return text.

Go for it.

She then drove back to the Davidson house, parked, and knocked. Dwight answered the door.

"Come in."

"Thank you."

He escorted her into the living room where Cynthia Davidson was sitting in one of the armchairs. She was young, not even as old as Sara, blond (probably natural), and would be pretty if she didn't look so tired. On her, the thinness that seemed to run in the family looked good. She was wearing jeans and what looked like it was one of Richard's old shirts, with her hair tied back with a band. She rose to greet Sara.

"I'm Cynthia."

"Special Agent FitzGerald. Nice to meet you."

Dwight started to sit down with them.

"I'm sorry, Mr. Davidson, but I need to speak to your sister alone."

"I don't think I like . . ."

"It's protocol. I'm sorry."

"It's all right, Dwight."

He stood indecisively for a moment, then went into the hall and up the stairs.

"He's used to looking after me."

"I understand. I've got big brothers myself."

"After our parents died, he was the one who took care of me. Richard was supposed to be the adult, be he was gone so much Dwight had to finish growing up faster than he wanted to and look out for his little sister."

"I understand. And I am sorry about Richard."

"Thank you. Dwight seems to be protecting me by sparing me the details. Can you tell me what really happened, please?"

"There are still lots of things we don't know, but basically, Richard apparently was spending the weekend at his hurricane house just off the beach. Sunday morning somebody came to the house, he evidently let them in, and they shot him. Several times. He died very quickly if that's any comfort."

"You said 'them.'"

"It appears there were two people. We have no idea who or why. That's why I'm here."

"And it wasn't a robbery."

"No."

"Some of his business partners?"

"The information we have so far indicates they are all worse off financially because of his death. Unless there is something unexpected in the will, if there is a will."

"There's a will somewhere. Mom and Dad had wills, even though they were a long way from old age, so Richard would have made one. I have one. I know Dwight has one. We'll find it eventually."

"You've been going through his things?"

"Yes. I dressed for the job."

"He had a cell phone and a laptop at the beach house when he was killed. By any chance have you run into another phone or laptop, or maybe a tablet or desktop, here at this house?"

"Richard was a typical nerd; he lived online. There's barely a sheet of paper in the house. He bought the best computer he could find, put everything on it, backed it up to the cloud, and then reformatted the hard drive of the old one and gave it to somebody at the office. The only documents I've found in the house so far are the leases he signed with somebody named Milton Roberts for the refreshment stands at the beach. And I guess those had to be in writing."

"Richard was, what, six years older than you? Yet you seem to have known him quite well."

"A little over six. But we were a close family. Frankly, my parents pretty much worked all the time. Richard was the one who did a lot of the actual childcare when we were kids."

"Tell me about him."

"Well, he was smart. Really, really smart. He started getting into computers even in his early teens. It became sort of an obsession. Except for running, he didn't do much of anything else. The med school idea came from our parents, who saw it more as a way to make a good living than actually caring for people. Frankly, he would have made a lousy doctor, at least if he had to deal with patients. Maybe medical research or something. When our parents died, he ditched the idea of medical school as soon as he could, and I don't blame him. But it gave him the idea for the electronic medical records software, so I guess all those pre-med courses had some use."

"Did he have many friends in high school or college?"

"Richard? No. No friends except a few other computer nerds, and most of those were only online friends. No friends, no enemies. Some of his teachers liked him because he was quiet and did good work, but that was it."

"No girlfriends?"

"Not as far as I know. He was just so much smarter than everybody else that it could be intimidating. He was confident enough at home, but he was very introverted, shied away from social stuff."

"Boyfriends?"

"You mean, like, gay? No way. No, forget that road, it's a dead end."

"On the laptop he had at the beach, he had some encrypted files. Any idea what might be on them?"

"Not a clue. But nothing sexual, you can forget that idea."

"He also had three email accounts, one for Meditrack, one for personal emails and the businesses at the beach, and a third one that we can't get into. Any idea what that account was used for?"

"No. Listen, Special Agent, my brother was many things, but he wasn't a pervert of some kind, or a spy, or anything like that. Yes, he was weird, but not in a bad way."

"Dwight seems to feel Richard never really understood what the two of you needed after your parents were killed. He seems to resent Richard using his position as guardian and executor to divert most of your inheritance into his business."

"Yeah, Richard didn't handle that well. It wasn't that he was mean, he just thought we were like him and didn't need anything besides food, shelter, and school. We both sort of had to get away from him to become whole people."

"Which Richard wasn't?"

"Let's say a very narrowly focused person. Some people are just like that, you know. Very smart, but only in certain areas. Not exactly an autistic savant but leaning in that direction. Hell, if you'd put a naked woman in front of him, I'm not sure he would have known what to do, but he could make a computer sing."

"Could that have made enemies? Women who felt rejected, perhaps?"

"Well, I never knew it to. He certainly didn't inspire love, Special Agent, but he didn't inspire hate either. He was just sort of tolerated, put up with because he was so good at what he did. He was brushed off as the strange one, not important enough to worry about."

"I see."

"If you don't have any more questions, I really need to get back to work. We both have to wrap this all up and get back to Arizona right after the funeral."

"Certainly. Just curious, but what will happen to this house?"

"You mean, assuming it's ours after the will is found?"

"Yes."

"Well, I certainly don't want it, or the beach house. Too many bad memories here, and I never want to go back to that beach again, that's for sure."

"Thank you for your time, Miss Davidson. Here's my card if you find anything or think of anything I might be interested in. We're doing everything we can to solve this."

"Thank you, but I'm not sure it makes much difference. Richard is dead. I just want to get back to Yuma."

"Well, thank you again."

And Sara was out the door, back in her car, and wondering where to go next. Eventually, she decided she needed an early lunch. She headed to Captain Stanley's Seafood on South Wilmington Street on the way back to the SBI offices and got the grilled fish combo plate just before the lunch rush hit. After eating, she went back to her car and called Butts to brief him on her meeting with Cynthia.

"Detective Butts."

"This is FitzGerald."

"I was just about to call you."

"What's up?"

"We finally found Davidson's car. It was in a commercial lot near one of the docks where you can rent docking spaces long-term. Nothing in it though besides the usual spare tire and a few tools. Owner's manual in the glove box. We also found the grocery where he bought his food. It's on the road just before you get into town. One of the cashiers said she saw him a few times a year, mostly in the summer and always on Friday nights. He would buy basically the same thing every time; milk, bread, coffee, cokes, cereal, peanut butter. Same as we found in the hurricane house. This guy is nothing if not consistent."

"Yeah."

"So, what have you got?"

"I talked to the sister. Brother didn't like me talking to her alone, but she seemed a little more relaxed with him out of the room. She says she has been going through Richard's stuff at the house, and no sign of another computer or phone or anything we didn't already know about. No sign of a will either, but they need a death certificate to get into the safe deposit box and look there."

"That shouldn't take too much longer now that the autopsy is done."

"She also basically repeated the line about Richard being obsessed with his computer work; no girlfriends, no boyfriends, no social life offline, but I'm not sure I'm buying this asexual stuff."

"Sounds a little weird to me too."

"I mean, he may have been sublimating his sex drive, or diverting it into the computer work, but he almost certainly had some kind of sex drive."

"Yeah."

"The question is, where was it popping up?"

"Well, I can't find anything here. Almost nobody down here even saw him, best I can tell. Cashier at the store, guy at the dock where he had the boat; that was about it. I found a couple of people who remember the family from the summers they worked here, but even then, they barely remember him except as the kid that ran the snow cone place. There was a little more memory of them as the kids whose parents were killed in the storm, but evidently, the three kids went back to Raleigh with their parents' bodies as soon as the bridge opened back up. That was the last most people here saw of them."

"That's not surprising. Dwight and Cynthia never want to see the beach again."

"Understandable, I guess."

"So why was Richard willing to go back? What makes him different?"

"More of a cold fish, maybe. Or only felt comfortable when he was in the hurricane house."

"Could be, but if I built a house on the beach and the beach disappeared from under it, that would seem like some kind of omen to me."

"He's a strange bird, any way you cut it."

"Listen, I think I'm going to go back to the software company, try to talk to a couple of the old hands who aren't the mucky-mucks, see if something oozes out around the edges."

"Sounds good to me. I'm trying to track down a couple of the former teenagers who worked for the family back in the day. See if they have anything to say."

"Good idea. I'll check back if I get anything."

"Go for it."

Sara drove to the Meditrack offices again and this time asked the receptionist for the employee who had been there the longest. After about ten minutes of watching people glancing at her without seeming to, she was led to a conference room inhabited by a woman in her thirties, dressed down in slightly below business casual, with new jeans, a plain t-shirt, denim jacket, and new-looking Nike's. Her hair was a mousy brown, cut straight at her shoulders, her face the definition of plain, her figure barely noticeable, and only her intelligent eyes were notable.

"Hello, I'm Carol Simmons. You asked to speak to the employee who has been here the longest, and I guess I'm it."

"Please sit. I'm SBI Special Agent FitzGerald."

"You want to know about Richard Davidson?"

"Yes, but let's back up a bit. First of all, what's your job here, and when did you join the company?"

"I'm a programmer. Head Programmer now. I write the actual computer code. Everything else is just plans and schemes until somebody puts it into a language the computer understands."

"OK."

"I was the fourth hire, about a year after Richard started working on the program. Richard was great at writing code, but it's a big program and there's just so much of it that he had to have help. The first three people he hired are long gone; there are a couple who came on in the year following me that are still here, but not many."

"Why is that?"

"Richard could be hard to work for. It wasn't that he was mean, he just didn't seem to understand that we had lives outside the job. He expected a little more than he should have."

"So why did you stay?"

"Well, I didn't have much of a life outside the job at the time. And, as I guess I don't have to tell you, jobs for women in male-dominated fields are a little hard to come by. I was also better at the job than most of them, which Richard noticed. I could get away with things the others couldn't because he needed me. Plus, once he hired Margaret Anderson to run the business side, things got more normal."

"Did the men hit on you?"

"Not Richard. Nor most of the others. I'm not exactly a sex goddess. There was one scum who tried a couple of things, until I broke his finger when I found his hand on my breast. He tried to raise a stink, but Richard just told him to type one-handed and keep his hands to himself. He left as soon as he could find another job. Once Margaret took over, she made it clear what wouldn't be allowed. No problems since."

"But you and Richard were close."

"We worked together. I needed the job; he needed a good programmer. We had each other's back, but it was never more than that."

"Was it ever more that that for Richard and anybody else?"

"Not that I know of. He worked late, he worked weekends, but mostly people tried to leave at normal times, not hang around to be alone with him. What he did outside the office, I have no idea. I did eventually develop a life outside the office, and nobody in the office was part of that."

"I see. Do you know if Richard was straight or gay?"

"Well, I never had any reason to think he was gay. I just assumed he was straight."

"Part of my problem here, Carol, is that I can't find any reason anybody would want to kill Richard Davidson. He was still a young man, a former athlete, yet everybody describes him as some sort of autistic eunuch who never did anything besides build software programs. And I'm having a little trouble buying that."

"Well, I see your problem, but nobody here wanted to kill him. He may have been an autistic eunuch, but he was our autistic eunuch, and we knew he was our gravy train."

"I understand the pay here was a little below norm."

"Yes, but we got a little share each year we worked here. When the profits started coming in, we got a payout each year."

"Big money?"

"Not really. Not even enough to make up for the low pay. But it was more each year, and there would have been a big payoff if we went public or got bought out or something like that."

"What were the chances of that happening?"

"I think they were getting pretty good. Margaret could tell you more about that than I could."

"You know, most men will at least look at women, glancing down at their breasts, watch their hips sway as they walk away. It's so common we hardly even notice it anymore. It's instinctive. It would almost seem strange if they didn't."

"I'm not saying Richard didn't look at women. I guess he did. He just never said or did anything about it here in the office."

"So why did somebody go to a lot of trouble to kill him?"

"I don't know, but it was either something at home or down on that beach, not here."

"Thank you for your time, Carol. Please take my card and call me if you think of anything."

"Sure. And I do hope you find who did this."

"So do I. So do I."

Sara decided this was enough of listening to the same story over and over again and went back to the office. She texted Butts, *I got zilch*. Then she spent the rest of the afternoon writing up reports on her interviews so far and left less than a half hour after quitting time.

Back in her apartment, she tossed a load in the washing machine and started on supper. She boiled up two cups of instant rice, and when that was done, she drained a can of little green peas and a can of tuna, then stirred those in with the rice until everything was warm. She then put the casserole into a microwavable dish, ate half of it while reviewing several of the news websites, preferring the ones that actually cared what was fact and what wasn't. She covered the remainder of her supper and put it in the refrigerator, took the clothes out of the washer, and put them into the dryer. She read a romance novel until the clothes were dry, folded and hung up as appropriate, and went back to wash the pot she cooked the rice in now that it had soaked for a while. Finally, she stripped her clothes off, performed her evening absolutions, watched the Braves game for half an hour, and then crawled into bed with herself and wandered around in her mind until she fell asleep.

Thursday

The next morning it was raining, so she just did a quick mile on the treadmill in the exercise room, then really worked out on the weight machines, both upper and lower body. Then back to her apartment to shower and dress for work.

She was barely back at her desk and logged in to her computer when the phone rang.

"Sara FitzGerald."

"Director Struber."

"Yes, sir."

"I just wanted to check in on that locked room case I gave you. How is that coming?"

"The locked room was a locked house, but that was the easy part. What we can't find is anybody with a motive to kill the victim. It wasn't a robbery, it wasn't random, and everybody seems to be worse off without the guy."

"Are we going to be able to crack this one?"

"I don't know, sir."

"You need anything from me?"

"I've already got the cyber team trying to crack a couple of passwords and decrypt some files, but they aren't giving me much hope."

"Well, keep at it a little longer. But sometimes we just have to move on, FitzGerald."

"Yes, sir."

He hung up, and Sara had barely hung up her phone when it rang again.

"FitzGerald."

"Butts."

"Man, I sure hope you've got something."

"Well, not really. Milt Roberts helped me contact three people who worked for the Davidsons their last summer. He hired them the next summer, so he had some contact info. They all said basically the same thing. They never got to know the Davidson kids because each one worked solo, manning a little refreshment stand by themselves twelve hours a day, every day. The hired help worked in shifts at the other stands. This was after the Davidsons were in their teens or older, of course, but that seems to be the pattern. The kids worked in the main stand until they were old enough to go it alone, while the hired teens were at other stands. So, nobody could tell me anything about Richard, or the other two for that matter."

"Oh, great."

"Listen, FitzGerald . . ."

"Yeah?"

"My chief is hinting I need to either make some progress on this or shove it to a back burner and pick up the other things on my desk. He doesn't like the idea of an unsolved murder on his beach, but we're a little department in a little town, and he needs me doing other things too."

"I get it. I'm getting the same kind of pressure at my end."

"I mean, if you know something else for me to do, I'll get it done, but I don't know what else to do unless somebody cracks some codes or some tip pops up."

"I know. Tell you what; I'll go canvas the neighbors on the Davidson block today. See if that gives us anything. You tackle your other cases for a while, and I'll get back to you if I find any trails to follow."

"Deal. Good luck."

"Thanks. I'll need it."

It had stopped raining by the time Sara parked on the street across from the Davidson house, but she pulled on her SBI-Police jacket to make herself readily identifiable. She walked to the house on the end of the block on the side across from the Davidsons' and started knocking on doors, working her way up the block. Where anybody was home at all it was usually an older housewife or a retired couple, with a few younger women with little kids mixed in. But the answers were always the same. A few had known the Davidsons before the parents were killed, more knew Dwight and Cynthia from when they lived there after the storm, but nobody really knew them well. The parents had been quiet, but hard workers who kept a nice yard, even hiring a neighborhood kid to cut the grass and pick up any litter during the summer when they were away at the beach, and it was so sad they were killed. Some said they had taken casseroles or cookies to Dwight and Cynthia from time to time since they seemed to be living close to the bone while in college.

Yes, they knew Richard lived there alone now, but they rarely saw him. He usually came home late, even on weekends, if he came home at all. No, they never saw any other cars in the driveway or people visiting. Richard kept to himself. But then he had been a quiet, serious person, even as a child. He kept the house looking nice and didn't bother anybody; he was just sort of there.

Sara had just finished the house next to the Davidson house when Dwight and Cynthia pulled into the driveway of their house. Seeing Sara, Cynthia got out of the car and walked down to meet her on the sidewalk.

"Were you looking for us?"

"No, just talking to some of the neighbors. Just routine canvasing. I think I can safely say Richard wasn't running drugs out of the house or hosting wild parties on weekends."

"No kidding."

"How are you doing?"

"Well, we finally got into the safety deposit box. Meditrack hired a lawyer because they need some clarity about the estate for some big business deal they are working on."

"And?"

"There was the will. Dwight and I are equal heirs, but Dwight is the executor. Guess Richard thought I still needed protecting by a big brother."

"Typical."

"Yeah."

"There is still probate to go through, and probably a lot of audits, before we get control of anything, but at least now we know. Frankly, I'm a little surprised Richard didn't put it into some kind of trust so somebody else would control the money for us, or mandate that it all go toward running one business or another, or something like that."

"You think you'll move back here and take control of the businesses?"

"No way in hell. You want to buy a house? It's a nice, quiet neighborhood."

"Thanks, but I suspect that would violate some ethics rule somewhere."

"Yeah, probably. We'll see if Milton Roberts still wants to buy the refreshment stands. If not, maybe we'll keep leasing them to him, as long as we don't actually have to go down to the beach. I don't know if anybody would buy the hurricane houses. I just hope Richard didn't still owe money on those."

"Guy at Carolina Beach named Harry Stiles, S-T-I-L-E-S, runs that business. He can tell you who did the last audit, maybe even provide a copy."

"Thanks, I'll check on that. But I bet the only business worth anything is Meditrack, and I have no idea what that might be worth. Did you meet Margaret Anderson there?"

"Yes."

"She seems to think they are on the verge of a big deal, but isn't sure it will go through now, without Richard. And having the estate all tied up in legal stuff won't help."

"Well, all I can do is wish you luck."

"Yeah, thanks. Will we ever find out who killed Richard?"

"Honestly, I don't know. We solve a lot of cases, but not all of them."

"Well, thanks for being honest about it. I better get back inside before Dwight makes any business deals without me."

"Right. Thanks for all the information."

"Sure."

And Cynthia walked back into the house. Sara went back to her car, decided to just skip lunch and go back to the office. She wrote up a summary of her conversations of the day, started to put an edited version into an email for Butts, but decided to call him instead.

"Butts."

"FitzGerald."

"Yeah."

"Just wanted to let you know they found the will. The brother and sister split the estate."

"Does that give them motive?"

"Well, I really don't think they were sure they were going to get it. And they still don't know how much it will be after all the debts are paid. Might not be a whole lot. Plus, we know they were in Arizona."

"Hired killer?"

"Possible, I guess. Not likely though, with so much unknown. And hired killers who can keep a secret can be hard to find outside the movies and the mafia. Plus, it sounds like the software business would have been worth a lot more if Richard was still alive when the buyout went through."

"So, what's next?"

"I think I'll drive down to the beach tomorrow. Just to look around. I just want to get a better idea of what it was like for Richard."

"Well, I'd love to be your guide, but my son has a Little League game tomorrow afternoon, and I've got piles of paper on my desk."

"No problem. I'm not looking for anything in particular. I just want to wander around, see the boardwalk and the refreshment stands. That shouldn't be hard to find, should it."

"Just park where you did before. We have a couple of spaces reserved for the department. Take one of those. Then walk toward the ocean. You can't miss it."

"I sure hope not. Missing a whole ocean would be embarrassing."

"Well, call me if you need me. I'll have my phone with me."

"Thanks. Enjoy the baseball."

"You've never seen a Little League game, have you?"

"No, can't say as I have."

"Well, let's just say parents do what they can for their kids. But sometimes they don't know when to stop."

"Got it."

Sara noticed it was past quitting time again, but she stayed long enough to file a travel form so she wouldn't have to come into the office in the morning before she left. Then she went home and ate the rest of the tuna, rice, and little green peas for supper. Checking the news websites and catching a little more of the Braves game took her up to bedtime. And thus ended the fourth day.

Friday

Morning came early. She wanted to get on the road, so just did a quick mile on the treadmill and a short upper-body workout, then showered and dressed. This time she wanted to blend in, so she went with some lightweight cotton pants that were just long enough to cover her ankle holster. She didn't want to bother with a lot of sunscreen, so she went with a long-sleeve white shirt with an open collar. Gym socks and the cross-trainers completed the outfit. She did get a stick of SPF seventy sunscreen and applied it to her neck, face, and the back of her hands, then tossed it in her backpack to reapply later.

Once she was far enough out of town that she didn't have to worry about rush-hour traffic, she stopped at a Krispy Kreme for a large coffee and a couple of donuts, then kept on trucking. Two hours later, she pulled into the parking lot by the docks and found the two parking spaces marked POLICE. She put her SBI sign on her dashboard, freshened up her sunscreen, hoisted her backpack, and crossed over to the little police booth on the dock. Seeing someone inside, she knocked and pulled the door open. It was the officer who had taken Butts and her out to the hurricane house.

"George, wasn't it?"

She glanced at his nametag. It said "Beasley."

"Ah, the SBI is back. What can I do for you, Special Agent?"

"Detective Butts said it would be OK if I parked in one of your reserved spaces."

"Yeah, sure, no problem. Is he meeting you?"

"No, his kid has a baseball game. I just want to look around anyway, get the lay of the land."

"You want to go out in the boat?"

"No, no. Just walk around town, see where things are."

"You want a map?"

"Thanks, but I have GPS on my phone."

"Sure."

"One thing I was wondering. On the Saturday before the murder, did anything unusual happen in town? You know, something out of the ordinary."

"You mean besides that girl going missing?"

"Butts mentioned something about that. What happened?"

"Around ten o'clock we got a call from the Hampton Inn. A couple was looking all over the beach for their fifteen-year-old daughter and couldn't find her anywhere. Well, you know the drill; missing tourist girl means all hands on deck. Doug Butts and I got in the dune buggy and drove the whole length of the beach, from the river up to the channel, showing her picture on his tablet to anybody still on the beach itself, asking if anybody had seen her. Eventually, one of the other uniforms found her drunk as a skunk and passed out in the HopLite Irish Pub up on the highway with a fake ID and Daddy's credit card in her pocket, but by then it was one o'clock in the morning. That was the only excitement on Saturday that I know of."

"You drove up to the end of the road?"

"Past it. With the dune buggy, we were actually on the beach itself, on the sand."

"And you went past the houses?"

"Sure. Sometimes people camp on the beach up there, even though they aren't supposed to. Kids will go up there past the lights to skinny dip or have sex on the beach. We don't usually patrol up there on a regular basis, but looking for the girl, we went all the way to the channel, even past where that hurricane house is."

"Was anybody on the beach up there?"

"Couple sacked out in a van, another couple asleep in a tent. We asked them about the girl first, then told them they had to move off the beach. They didn't give us any problem, though they weren't happy."

"I guess not. Did you see any lights in the hurricane house?"

"Not that I remember, though by then it was really late, well past midnight. His boat may have been there, but I'm not sure. We were sweeping the beach with the searchlight, but not the ocean. But there wasn't anybody else on the beach then. We made sure of that. We were on our way back down the beach when we got the call the girl had been found. It was after two before we could get back to the station and shut things down for the night. Chief gave everybody he could the next morning off so we could get a little shuteye. Not much happens on Sunday morning anyway; even some of the tourists go to church."

"You ever see Richard Davidson around town, or even on the beach anywhere?"

"The victim? No. I knew somebody was using that steel house occasionally because I would see the boat tied up when I went by in the boat to patrol the beach, but I never laid eyes on him before we found the body, far as I know."

"Well, thank you, George."

"You decide you want to go out on the boat, just let me know."

"Thanks. I appreciate that. But right now, I just want to walk around. Which way is the boardwalk?"

"Go around the end of the harbor to Canal Street, go a block south, then follow your ears to the ocean."

"Sounds good, thanks."

She followed his directions, and soon found herself on the north end of the boardwalk with the beach on one side and several blocks of shops on the other. The beach had some people on it, but not as many as would be there later in the day. There were also window shoppers along the shops, but not really a crowd. She was passing the door of a beachwear shop with mannequins in the windows wearing bikinis that no sane woman would dare actually wear in the water when she literally bumped into Milt Roberts coming out the door.

"Excuse me. Ah, Agent Fitzpatrick."

"FitzGerald."

"Well, I was close. What brings you back to our fair city?"

"Just looking around. Seems like a nice beach."

"Well, we like it."

"This one of your stores?"

"Actually, yes. See anything you like?"

"Frankly, Mr. Roberts, I would be amazed if you had anything in my size."

"You know, Miss FitzGerald, thinking about it, I would be too. I do have another store, a couple of blocks off the beach, that has a wider range of sizes and styles, including mix-and-match tops and bottoms. I'd be happy to walk over there with you and see if we can't accommodate you."

"Thanks. Maybe some other time. But you know what would help me?"

"I am at your service."

"Can you point out the refreshment stands the Davidsons used to run? I'm trying to get an idea of what growing up here in the summer was like for them. You run them now, right?"

"Yes. Sure. The grand tour."

He walked down the boardwalk to the first corner. On the corner was a little, maybe ten-foot by ten-foot, building, open above waist level on two sides, with metal shutters that could be rolled down to close the openings. Boxes of fudge and salt-water taffy lined the counters, with a couple of little sample trays out to lure people to stop. A couple of teenagers were inside, one busy pouring out a sheet of fudge on a back table to cool and be cut.

"This is the main stand, where the parents worked and kept the kids until they were old enough to take over a stand on their own. The next one is just two doors down across the side street."

He took her to a smaller stand that only had an open counter on one side since it wasn't on a corner. It was a shaved ice snow cone stand, with the ice shaving machine and a couple dozen bottles of flavoring syrup carefully lined up on the counter. It was barely bigger than a closet, seemingly inset into a little space carved out of a larger souvenir shop, and had a real window as the opening instead of something bigger. A buck-toothed girl who looked barely old enough to be working was alone in this booth.

Three more shops down the block, Milt pointed out a cotton candy booth. It had two of those spinner things that spun the sugar and dye into cotton candy. There were several colors of cotton candy spun onto a paper stick, most covered in plastic bags, though you could get a fresh one right from the spinner if you were willing to wait a few seconds and take whatever flavor was being made at the time. The boy with acne operating this one sat on a tall stool since there didn't seem to be room for a chair. Very similar were the soft-serve ice cream place and the soft-drink stand. The popsicle place wasn't even a booth, just a little architectural nook created by two buildings not being even with each other where a bored teen stood behind a little freezer chest on wheels with a sign listing today's flavors taped on the front. By the time they got to the popcorn booth, they were almost to the end of the boardwalk.

"And that's it, the seven sites I lease from the Davidsons. As for what it was like for them, I can't imagine. It's hard enough to find kids who will sit around like that for five hours, and they have cell phones to play with. I have to walk around several times a day checking to see who's getting into trouble."

"They work five-hour shifts?"

"My hires do. I just keep the stands open from ten to eight; the Davidsons kept going until ten at night. I split the shifts into two five-hour shifts a day, six days a week, for thirty hours, then have a couple of floaters to cover for people on their days off, which rotate so not everybody is off the same days. Technically that makes it part-time and I don't have to pay benefits. It's the only way to make a profit on these things. The Davidsons worked their kids twelve hours a day, seven days a week. They were blood, so the labor laws didn't apply, what there were back then. But I still think it was child abuse."

"I see what you mean."

"It's depressing just thinking about it. But nobody was in a position to say anything about it."

"Did you say Detective Butts's daughter worked for you last summer?"

"Yeah, Eliza. Good kid. No trouble from her. She had two girlfriends who also worked for me. They would text each other all day, then get together after they got off at eight and go do whatever sixteen-year-old girls do to blow off steam."

"In Texas that was talk about boys and chase cattle in an ATV. I'm guessing there was not much cattle chasing around here."

"No, and I'm not sure what the beach equivalent would be."

"Not sure myself."

"It's still a little early for lunch, Miss FitzGerald, but I'd be happy to get you a free ice cream or snow cone or whatever. Maybe give you a chance to talk to one of the teens working for me, if that would help."

"Thank you, Mr. Roberts, but I want to walk up to the hurricane house before it gets hot. I want to see what things look like from the beach side."

"OK, well, you go back to the other end of the boardwalk, cut through the Hampton Inn, and come out on Carolina Avenue. You follow that until you get to the fishing pier, where that road runs out. But if you go one block up, you get on Canal Drive, which will go about another long block before it peters out. Or you can just go around the end of the pier and keep on going. After that, there is just beach up until you hit the channel where it opens into the ocean. You can't miss the house; it's all by itself out there. But that's quite a hike. Mile and a half, maybe two miles. Be easier to drive up Canal Drive and park near the pier if you didn't want to take your car out onto the sand."

"I think I'd like to walk. Really see what's here."

"Mostly residential up that way; take a bottle of water with you."

"Thank you for the directions and advice, Mr. Roberts. And I appreciate the tour."

"Always happy to help."

So she set off back up the boardwalk, stopping to get a bottle of cold water out of a machine, which she slipped in her backpack, then stopping at the snow cone booth for a large, grape-shaved ice snow cone. Finding the street that ran right along the beach, with only one row of houses between street and beach was easy, and she marveled at both the wide variety of houses and mailboxes along the street, as well as at how close the houses were to each other. Beachfront property must cost a pretty penny.

There seemed to be two informal community contests going on, one for the cutest mailbox. While they all started with regulation mailboxes, they were decorated within an inch of illegality. Some only had beach or nautical scenes spray-painted on the sides, but others had miniature working windmills on top and others were encased in fiberglass cases that resembled giant large-mouth fish and various other ocean-related enhancements. The other competition seemed to be for the most clever name for the beach cottage. Each dwelling not only had an address, but each had a name, usually on a rustic wooden plaque mounted over the garage door. These titles ranged from the stereotypical "Fair Harbor" or "Stephen's Rest," to the more daring "Tax Shelter 2" or "Wilson's Revenge."

At intervals, there was a cross street that dead-ended at a wooden walkway over the sand dunes, with a sign at the end proclaiming PUBLIC BEACH ACCESS, with signs on either side of the street announcing, NO PARKING. Basically, it was beach access for people who lived on the other side of the street.

Sara had long since finished the snow cone and had been looking for a trash can to deposit the paper cup for three blocks when she reached the fishing pier, which had a convenient trash can outside the building you had to go through to get onto the pier. She paused to get rid of her trash and dig the no-longer-cool bottle of water out of her backpack. There was a small beach on each side of the pier, but past that was the breakwater, with large blocks of stone piled in a line running from up on the beach well out into the water.

Rather than scramble over the blocks, she turned left and went a short block to Canal Drive, then turned back parallel to the beach. Here the houses thinned out, leaving vacant lots even before she reached the end of the road. There was a barrier across the road, but even as she watched, a car approached the barrier, turned onto the sand, and went around the barrier, pulling back onto what was left of the old road, now covered with a layer of sand. Past the breakwater, the beach narrowed, leaving a much thinner strip of sand between the water and the natural dunes. Some of the dunes were low enough that she could glimpse scrub brush and marsh on the other side. Somewhere back over there was the channel they had sailed up from the harbor to get around the end of the island to the hurricane house, but she didn't want to see that enough to climb a dune. It was probably not a good idea to disturb the sea grass holding the dune in place anyway.

Besides, she was here for other reasons. She kept walking, sipping her water now and then. There were a few people on the beach, but that population decreased rapidly, replaced now and then by a jeep or small pick-up truck parked near the dunes and a fisherman standing on the edge of the water, casting as far as he could into the surf, then sticking his two or three long poles' handles into the sand and waiting until he saw a pole twitching with a fish on the end of the line. She also occasionally noticed a set of pilings out in the water, but since it appeared to be high tide, they weren't sticking up much.

Continuing on, she finally caught sight of the hurricane house, isolated in the water, about half a football field from shore. Coming even with it, she could see the cut-through channel at the end of the beach that led from the sea to the harbor. She realized it would be easy to swim to the house, especially at low tide, and made a mental note to check the tide tables for last Saturday night and Sunday morning. She looked back in the direction she had come and saw the end of the fishing pier, but it was so far away she doubted anybody on the pier could have seen anything happening here on the beach. She also realized that with no houses or other buildings anywhere around and no streetlights, it would have been very dark here at night. Maybe even Texas-prairie dark. There was not a lot she missed about Texas, but she did miss the sky full of stars at night, not the pitiful imitation of a sky visible through all the city light pollution. Yes, this place might be beautiful at night. And she saw what George had meant about this being a good place for skinny-dipping or sex. Made her wonder what might have been seen from the hurricane house.

Having seen what she came to see, she headed back down the beach, gradually returning to civilization, good or bad. She stopped again at the pier to put her plastic bottle in a recycling bin and buy another bottle of water. This time she walked back along Canal Drive, which ran alongside the canal to the harbor. It was pretty much the same as Carolina Avenue had been as far as the houses were concerned, except on one side the houses backed into the canal and all had little docks.

By the time she got back to the end of the harbor and was able to go around to her car, it was past lunchtime. She stopped to use the public restroom just off the parking lot and put her empty water bottle in another recycling bin. She avoided the police boat dock in case George Beasley was there, got in her car, and drove out of town. Once she was across the bridge on 421 and off the island, she started looking for a restaurant, but it was several miles up the road toward Wilmington before she found a seafood restaurant that Yelp approved of.

A fried fish platter and some banana pudding later, she was on the road again. By the time she pulled into the Raleigh area, it was evening, but she stopped at the neighborhood Publix to do her weekly grocery shopping. Once home, she made sure she had gotten all the sand off and out of her shoes, unloaded the groceries and put them away, and took her .32 out of the ankle holster and gave it a thorough cleaning. Finally, she stripped, showered, and crawled into bed, not liking the thoughts she was thinking.

Saturday

Saturday was her running day. She skipped the weight room and went straight to the nearby jogging path. She ran out for an hour, then back for another hour, not counting distance, not pushing the pace, just working on technique, trying to make her stride as effortless as possible. Back at the apartment, she showered and pulled on some old jeans and a western-style shirt still hanging in there from her days in Texas.

She fixed herself a big plate of pancakes with blueberry syrup, a hot cup of coffee, and a big glass of ice water for breakfast. After eating, she did a little house cleaning, put on her usual armament, and went into the office. Once logged in to the official computer network, she accessed the vital records for the various New England states one at a time until she found the record she was looking for. Now knowing which state to look in, she started digging into other public records until she thought she finally knew what happened.

By then it was supper time, so she collected her printouts from the printer, locked them in her desk, and headed out. In no hurry to get back to her apartment and not having eaten since the pancakes at breakfast, she stopped at Cocula Tex-Mex restaurant for a meal that sort of resembled a taste of home cooking. At least the fish tacos were decent, and it was hard to mess up black beans. And cooking was one of the skills she was still working on, so eating out was usually a good thing.

Once back at the apartment, she fiddled around with cleaning a little more, but soon gave that up, undressed, and flipped on the Braves game.

Sunday

Sunday was weight day. She went to the exercise room and worked on upper and lower body machines, trying to add just a few pounds to each weight over her previous total, then getting in enough reps to build endurance as well as strength. Breakfast this time was high protein; ham slices, eggs, milk. Today she went with a dress, blending in with all the churchgoers in town. But she went back to the office to work on that report for the Director that had been put on the back burner by the beach case.

About mid-afternoon, she stopped working long enough to send Butts a text. *May have something. Can you come up tomorrow morning?* The reply came a few minutes later. *Nine o'clock OK?*

To this, she responded, *No hurry. Whenever.* Back came, *See you between ten and eleven.*

Good, she responded, then went back to working on the report.

She knocked off in time to be home for supper. She got a box of macaroni and cheese mix from the cabinet, boiled the water, put in the pasta from the mix and a little more from a plain box of pasta, let that boil the recommended time, drained the water, and put in the cheese powder, the milk, and the margarine as on the box directions, then added some extra sharp cheddar and a big chunk of Swiss cheese. When all that was melted together, she served it up and checked CNN-Headline news to see if the world had ended.

The world had not ended, but the Braves had played in the afternoon, so she checked the PBS channel and ended up watching some tour of the castles in Britain. When that got too boring, she picked up her romance novel and tried to see whose bodice would be ripped next. Eventually, even that became too boring, so she just shut everything down and went to bed to dream of her own bodice being ripped.

The Second Monday

Sara woke up before the alarm clock rang. She pulled on her workout clothes and went to the exercise room, but barely got in two miles on the treadmill before calling it off for the day. Breakfast was a couple of bagels and some coffee. Today she wanted to look official, so she went with the knee-length blue skirt and a white shirt and a matching blue jacket, with the usual accessories.

She got into the office early to go over her files on the case. At nine o'clock she had her regular weekly meeting with her immediate supervisor, the Special Agent in Charge of the Raleigh region. After the meeting, she reserved an interrogation room and went to sit at her desk. By 10:45, she was beginning to wonder if Butts was going to make it, but then the phone rang.

"This is the reception desk. A Detective Butts is here to see you."

"Good. Make him put his weapons in a locker and then wand him. I'll be right down."

By the time she got downstairs, the guard was running the metal-detector wand up and down Butts's body. The guard gave her a nod and let Butts cross to her.

"You guys don't take any chances."

"Just procedure. You know how it is these days."

"No kidding."

She took him up to the field agent's floor and escorted him to the interrogation room. As he walked in, the red light on the camera came on.

"Hey, what is this?"

"It's just a few questions."

"You're recording this? What's going on, FitzGerald?"

"I just have a few questions."

"What am I, some kind of suspect?"

"Please, Doug, just sit down."

He sat reluctantly.

"Do I need a lawyer?"

"You know the rules as well as I do, Doug. You're not under arrest; you can get up and leave. Or, if you have the name of a lawyer, I'll give them a call and we can wait until they get here. Or, I can get a public defender in here in about half an hour. But I hope you'll just answer my questions. Do you want a lawyer?"

"Just tell me what this is about."

"Am I going to have to exhume the body of your grandchild in order to get a DNA sample proving that Richard Davidson is his father?"

She watched the expressions run across his face. First came surprise, then a little shock. Next, the mental wheels started turning. How much does she know? How did she find out? Have I underestimated this big bitch? If I say yes, what does that imply? What if I say no? Should I try to walk out? Would they stop me? He tried to think three, four, five moves down the chess game, and didn't like any of the possibilities. She waited a whole minute for him to speak, but he just looked at her.

"Let me help you, Doug. On March 28 your daughter Eliza

May Butts gave birth to a son in Burlington, Vermont. She named him Douglas Earl Butts. The father was listed as 'Unknown.' He was scheduled to be adopted, but he had some health problems and died the next day. Your daughter became severely depressed and is still under psychiatric care."

"He didn't even live a whole day. It was a heart defect. Not even twelve hours."

"But Richard Davidson was the father."

Again, there was a long pause.

"Doug, please, don't make me dig up a little baby."

He finally looked down at the table between them.

"Yes."

"Yes, Richard Davidson is the father?"

"Yes, Richard Davidson is the father."

"Do you want that lawyer now?"

He was silent.

"Doug?"

"Just get on with it."

"Let's do it this way. I'll tell you a story, and you correct me if I get anything wrong. Last summer, in late June, your daughter and two of her friends drove out to the end of the beach after getting off work at Milt Roberts's refreshments stands at eight on a Friday or Saturday night. It was dark, they thought they were alone; they wanted some little adventure, so they decided to go skinny dipping. Usually, the police patrol doesn't go out that far, but for some reason that night the dune buggy patrol came along. Either Eliza was out in the water, or she didn't want to be recognized by some of your cop friends . . ."

"It's hard being a cop's daughter."

"I'm sure. Whatever the reason, instead of coming back on shore and getting caught in the searchlight, she swam out to the little dock on the hurricane house. The other two girls, not wanting to give her away, snatched up all the clothes and ran to the car, caught in the searchlight all the way. They hopped in the car and took off, planning to come back and pick up Eliza after the police left. But the cops started scanning the water to see if there was anybody else, and when Richard Davidson opened his door to see what all the lights were about, Eliza ran up the stairs and into the house, naked as a jaybird. For whatever reason, Richard didn't signal the cops. Right so far?"

"Close enough."

"The two girls drove down to the pier parking lot and waited for the cops to drive by. It's the only way off the beach. But they didn't come and they didn't come, and when they finally did drive up, they started doing a scan of the parking lot, and the girls had to haul out and drive all the way back to town before they were sure they weren't being followed.

"But they had Eliza's cell phone in the car, along with her purse and clothes. They pretended to be her and texted her mother that they were having some car problems or something and would be in late. Then they sent the same excuse to their parents. They waited as long as their nerves would let them, then drove slowly back to the beach, looking for cops behind every dune. By now it had been hours. And when they got back to where they had left Eliza, she wasn't there.

"They called, they yelled, they blew the car horn, but no Eliza. By now, there was no boat at the hurricane house and no lights, so it never occurred to them that Eliza had swum out there. They were just about to panic and call the police when they got a text from Eliza's sister's phone, but from Eliza, saying not to worry about her, that she was home. Richard Davidson had given Eliza a boat ride back to the harbor, right? And she walked home wearing a pair of his gym shorts and a sweatshirt he gave her."

"We would have recognized those were not her clothes if we had seen them, but she tapped on her sister's window and was tossed some of her own clothes before she came to the front door and woke us up."

"And you let her have it big time for being so late."

"Grounded her. She would have to come in right after work for two weeks. We were not happy."

"The other two girls also got in trouble with their parents, no doubt."

"Yes."

"But the next morning, there they were at the door, smuggling in Eliza's purse and clothes right under your nose."

"Yes."

"But a few weeks later she figures out that she is pregnant, and the whole truth comes out."

"Yes."

"Doug, what happened in that hurricane house?"

"Well, she got pregnant, so it's pretty obvious what happened."

"Was Eliza raped?"

"He was thirty years old. She was barely sixteen. What would you call it?"

"The age of consent in North Carolina is sixteen."

"Which is totally stupid."

"But legally, unless she was forced, it was just two consenting adults. Was she forced?"

"She says no, but I don't know if that's true or if she was just afraid of what I would do if she said yes. She knows what happens to women who make a rape accusation, even if it's true. I think she was more afraid of the courts and all that."

"What do you think happened?"

"I don't know. She would never talk about it. About what happened in the hurricane house. Shame, I guess. I don't know what happened. I just know the result."

"And Baptists don't believe in abortion."

"Well, this Baptist doesn't."

"But a deacon of the church, a pillar of the community, having a pregnant, unmarried sixteen-year-old daughter wouldn't work either, even in this day and age, would it?"

"Not exactly."

"So you sent her off to some 'home' in Vermont until all this is over with."

"It's a private boarding school. Good school, actually. They just accept girls in complicated situations and arrange adoptions."

"Except this baby died, and Eliza didn't handle all this very well."

"No."

"Is she going to be OK?"

"I hope so. Eventually. She just needs some time and a little help."

"Well, I really hope things work out for her."

"Thank you."

"Jumping forward almost a year, Saturday night a week ago, you and George Beasley are driving the beach looking for that missing girl. When you get to the end of the beach you notice that there is a boat tied up at the hurricane house. The next morning, you stay in bed until your family leaves for church. Then you get up, go down to the police dock. You know nobody will be there because the Chief gave as many people as possible the morning off after the late night. You take the boat out to the hurricane house, tie up, flash your police badge through the window, and Richard Davidson opens the door."

"Yes."

"Then what?"

"I go in, introduce myself as Eliza's father, tell him he has become a father himself, but that his child has died."

"And?"

"I will never, ever, repeat what he said about Eliza, but it was the wrong thing to say."

"So?"

"So I shot him."

"But not with your service pistol."

"I had two drop guns."

"By drop guns you mean guns you had confiscated over the years from suspects, but not turned in as evidence? Guns that could not be traced back to you that could be dropped at the scene of a shooting if needed to make it look like someone who had been shot had been carrying a gun?"

"Yes."

"I've seen you eat, Doug. You're ambidextrous."

"Yes. I had a gun in each hand. Made it look like two gunmen."

"Then?"

"Then I gloved up, picked up the shell casings, locked up all the shutters and doors from the inside except the window by the door, got some ice from the freezer, climbed out the window, closed the window, jammed the ice where it would hold up the shutter bar until it melted, and then closed the shutter with the bar held up by the ice, and left."

"Why go to all that trouble?"

"I wanted to make it look complicated. Give me an excuse not to solve it."

"You didn't expect your Chief to call the SBI."

"I didn't expect you would figure it out."

"So you get back in the boat and . . ."

"Swing out to sea a little ways, toss the guns and put the shell casings and gloves in a weighted bag, and toss that over the side too."

"Then back to the dock, home, undress, and be sitting there in your pajamas when the family gets home."

"Yes."

"Douglas Butts, you are under arrest for the murder of Richard Davidson. You have the right . . ."

"Yeah, yeah, yeah, I know my rights. I waive my rights. I waive everything. You've got your recorded confession. Just get this over with."

Sara stood and collected her case file.

"I'm sorry, Doug."

"Yeah, yeah. You know parents; you do what you can for your kids."

"But sometimes you don't know when to stop."

The door to the interrogation room opened and a uniformed officer stepped inside. Sara's Special Agent in Charge was in the hall, having watched through the one-way mirror.

"Good job, FitzGerald. We'll get him over to lockup and make sure he calls his wife. I'll let the Director know to call the Chief in Carolina Beach."

"I'll start on the report right now."

She went back to her desk. It was lunchtime, but she wasn't hungry, and there was lots of paperwork to do. She wondered why it was still called paperwork when it was now done on computer. She realized she would never find out what was in the encrypted documents on Richard Davidson's computer or what was in the third email file. Nor would she find out what Richard Davidson said to Doug Butts that set him off, or what really happened the night naked Eliza Butts ran into Richard Davidson's hurricane house.

But by the end of the afternoon, her part of the case would be done and it would be the District Attorney's Office's job to take over. Then, she could finally get to the crime distribution data analysis for the Director. If she worked a little overtime, she could have that done by the end of the week. Then, maybe she could take the weekend off. Go somewhere. Maybe the mountains. Ashville was supposed to be nice this time of year. Or Smokey Mountain National Park. Away from the beach.

The River

Detective Carlos Ruffin of the Chesapeake, Virginia, Department of Police, stood in the middle of the small pier and looked at the empty spot at the end of it where a man had been killed with nobody anywhere close to him. He shivered as a cold winter wind blew off the river. He glanced at the one-paragraph hospital report that said the man, Elmer Munson, thirty-one, had been picked up by an ambulance crew and transported to Chesapeake General Hospital from this pier the day after Christmas, where he was pronounced dead. Then he reviewed the preliminary coroner's report. Any death with no known cause required an autopsy. Evidently, the coroner had assumed drug use, a heart problem, or a stroke, but when the autopsy didn't show any needle marks in the usual places, a heart defect, or evidence of a brain hemorrhage, he had taken a more careful look. The coroner had then found a small needle mark on Munson's neck, an unusual place for an injection. This had led to collecting samples for a drug screening and a phone call to the police department. The chain reaction led to Detective Ruffin standing on this little pier, reviewing the slim file.

He looked around at the pier. It had no railings and was only about thirty yards long, just long enough to lead from the shore, over the row of big rocks lining the shore to prevent erosion, and out just far enough to have a few feet of water at the end even when the James River was low, and the tide was out. Looking over the river, he saw where the James met the body of water called Hampton Roads, which in turn opened to the Chesapeake Bay. There were several big ships and a few smaller boats well offshore, mostly staying in the channel near the middle of the big river. Far away, he could just make out the city of Hampton on the opposite shore.

To both right and left, he saw the river lapping against the riprap protecting the shoreline and a much larger pier off in the distance to his left. Turning around, he saw the small road running parallel to the shore where his car was parked. Beyond that was a series of long buildings, identical in size and shape, spaced carefully far apart and lined up in rows, with what looked like the remnants of old railroad spurs running beside them.

Just then, something that looked like a police car but was labeled "Campus Police" pulled up and parked behind his car. A man in a sort-of police uniform got out with a file folder and walked over to the detective.

"Detective Ruffin?"

Carlos presented his badge and ID. The man extended his hand and they shook.

"I'm Charlie Hough, head of campus security. Nice to meet you."

"You used to be with the County Sheriff's Department."

"Does it show somehow?"

"I think I've heard the name. I was with the South Norfolk police before the incorporation."

What they both knew and didn't need to say was that about a year earlier, back in 1962, a hotshot lawyer living in a suburb just outside the Norfolk and Portsmouth city limits, not pleased by either city's annexation plans, had discovered a loophole in state law that allowed for an entire county to incorporate into a city easier than the usual legal process. The lawyer had organized a group of like-minded tax resisters and, suddenly, in 1963, the whole county of Norfolk (including a major section of the Great Dismal Swamp) and the little city of South Norfolk had become the giant city of Chesapeake. At least, it was a giant if you only counted square miles inside the city limits. Running from the North Carolina border all the way to the shores of Hampton Roads, it was now the biggest city in Virginia and the seventeenth biggest in the entire United States. In the process of converting from a county to a city, the Sheriff's Department had practically been eliminated as part of creating the new city police force. But in the transition, some of the law enforcement higher-ups had tried to eliminate the deadwood, troubled cops, and political opponents. Which one Charlie Hough had been, Detective Ruffin wasn't sure, but he knew Charlie was too young to have retired with full service and moved on to the cushy job of chief of campus security. Meanwhile, Patrol Officer Ruffin had taken advantage of the confusion and a talent for taking written police exams to move up to the lowest slot on the detective ladder.

"So, Carlos Ruffin, is it? You don't look Hispanic."

"Family name. Technically it's Carlos Leroy Ruffin IV. Nobody's sure how it got started. We're all from eastern North Carolina as far back as we can trace. But my father and grandfather were proud enough of it to pass it down, so I try to do right by it."

"Makes sense. So, you're here about the death?"

"The coroner has asked us to clear up some details."

"Well, I was off that day, right after Christmas, you know. My officer that handled it is off today, but I brought you a carbon of his report."

Chief Hough handed Carlos the thin folder. He took it and put it with the other reports he had without even looking at it. Gesturing toward the rows of buildings, Carlos asked, "What is this place?"

"Oh, yeah, I guess it does look strange if you're not used to it. It used to be a Marine Corps munitions depot. The offices and barracks were all on the other side of the base, beyond that line of trees. These were the warehouses, for the bombs and ammunition. They were spaced out like this so if one exploded it wouldn't take the whole base up with it. Anyway, back around 1960, a guy named Fred Beasley bought it as military surplus. He had made a pile, a big pile, in icehouses, construction, and God knows what else. His son had been killed in a car accident, so he didn't have anybody to leave all his money to.

"So, he decides to spend some of those millions opening a college for people who can't afford to go to college. He basically pays tuition for most of the students. This became the campus. Barracks became dorms, offices became classrooms, mess halls became dining halls. But he was trying to do all this on the cheap, so instead of paying full salaries to the faculty and administrators, he converted these warehouses into duplex apartments. Faculty get a free apartment and free meals when the dining hall is open. And not much actual money.

"Anyway, all the professors and administrators live out here. Most of them are gone right now for the holidays, especially with the dining hall closed. Munson, the guy who died, lived down there, the second apartment in the second building in that row. The Covingtons, the people who called it in, live in the first row, first building, second apartment. You can see it's easy for any of them to just walk over here to fish or whatever."

"So what did your man tell you?"

"About three o'clock the day after Christmas he got a call from Mrs. Covington saying her boys had come home yelling that Mr. Munson had collapsed on the pier. She said Mr. Covington had walked over to check on him, but she wanted Security to come help. Anyway, he jumped in his car and drove over. Covington had Munson stretched out on the pier, but it was obvious he was dead.

"My officer radioed back to the office for them to call an ambulance, then stayed with the body until the ambulance came and took Munson to the hospital to make it all official. Took about twenty minutes for the ambulance to get there. Anyway, that's when the office called me at home, and I started calling around for the dean or the president, but they were both out of town for the holidays. Finally, I got hold of the dean's secretary, and she had emergency phone numbers. They sent somebody to the hospital, I'm not sure who, to handle that paperwork and roused somebody in personnel to find out the next of kin. What I heard was that his mother was listed, but she had died just a month ago and the file hadn't been updated yet. I think they're still trying to find out who's next of kin."

"Did you know Munson?"

"Just to recognize. I'd had to talk to him a few times about security and crowd control around his play productions. Neither one was really a problem; they got some students and faculty to show up, but not anything near capacity in the auditorium. I didn't care for him that much, you know, an unmarried theatre guy, but it wasn't a problem."

"You think he was a homosexual?"

"Well, I couldn't say for sure. Just like I said, thirty-plus years old, never married, directing plays and such. We never got any complaints though."

Carlos didn't say anything about his being in his thirties and unmarried. He had had a series of girlfriends over the years, but one by one they had decided he was not the man they wanted to spend their life with. They had all moved on to other people. Carlos wasn't sure what about him was not acceptable and sometimes wondered.

"You check his apartment?"

"Got a locksmith to come out the next day to get us in. One of the English professors and I went in to make sure the gas was off and there weren't any dogs or cats that needed feeding. Checked his desk and whatever was on it for any information on relatives but didn't really toss the place. Did find some envelopes with his mother's address, but personnel already had that. Put everything back where it came from. Sealed it up and put a padlock on the door. If you want to get in, stop by the security office at the main gate and whoever's there can let you in and stay until you leave. I've got to get to a meeting on the other side of campus, if that's OK."

Carlos noticed movement in the distance and saw a man walking toward them.

"Who's that?"

"Oh, that's W. T. Covington. Math professor and the man

who was on the pier with the body when my man got there. You want to talk to him?"

"Sounds like a very good idea."

Hough yelled over to him. "Hey, Mr. Covington, this is a detective from the police department. He's trying to clear up some stuff about Mr. Munson. Can you talk to him for a few minutes?"

Covington waved and kept walking toward the pier.

"Like I said, I've got to go, if you need anything else, just stop at the campus security office. Nice meeting you, Detective."

"Thanks for the time,"

Charlie Hough got in his patrol car and drove away just as W. T. Covington made it to the pier.

"Mr. Covington, I'm Detective Ruffin of the Chesapeake Police Department. You're the math teacher?"

"Nice to meet you. Yes, one of the math department. You're here about poor Munson?"

"Just clearing up some details. I understand you found the body. Could you tell me about it, and please go into as much detail as possible?"

"Actually, I guess it was my boys who found the body. I've got one who just turned thirteen, and ten-year-old twins. They were out here playing on the rocks after lunch that day. You know how boys are."

"I'm told I used to be one."

"Yeah, well, they said they saw Mr. Munson walk over from his house with his fishing gear and stuff. Said he waved to them as he walked out onto the pier. Normally, they would have been roaming all over out here. It's a closed campus and all, so it's about as safe as can be. But Munson had one of those portable transistor radios, you know, the new little ones. He had it on one of the trashy rock and roll stations, so they hung around the area to hear the music, the Beatles and all that junk. We don't let them listen to it at home, so they were curious."

"Sure. Boys and all."

"Right. Evidently, Munson set up his camp stool and stuff and went to fishing. After a while, one of them looked up and saw Munson had collapsed out of the chair and was lying on the pier, not moving or anything. The boys were still out on the rocks. They're not allowed out on the pier without me or my wife, but the older one went onto the pier far enough to see something was wrong. He told the twins to run home and get somebody. When they told me and my wife that Mr. Munson had fallen out of his chair on the pier and wasn't moving, I told her to call security and then trotted over to see what was going on."

"And what did you find?"

"When I got here, the older boy and I went out the rest of the way onto the pier. By the time I got there, Munson was already dead. I don't know how long it was between the time he died and the time my boys noticed him out of his chair, but he was long gone. He was on his side next to the chair, so I rolled him over onto his back, checked his pulse, even listened to his chest. His eyes were open, so I held my hand over them to see if his pupils would react to changes in light, and there was nothing. So, I turned that trashy radio off and told my boy to run home, make sure security was coming, and then keep everybody in the house. A couple minutes later, the security guard rolls up, comes over, and does the same checks I did, goes back to his car for a minute, then comes back here. We just stand there until the ambulance arrives. Didn't even talk much except to agree that Munson was dead, and that he was awful young to have a heart attack. Eventually, the ambulance arrives. Seemed to take a long time, but I guess at that point it didn't matter. The ambulance attendants agree he's dead but take him off to the hospital anyway so there'll be a doctor to sign the death certificate."

"Was there anybody else around the area?"

"I didn't see anybody, and my boys said there wasn't anybody. This is the faculty ghetto, and pretty much everybody is gone for the holidays, visiting family and all. We're from Arkansas and didn't have the money for that long a trip this year."

"What about boats? Were there any boats around?"

"None anywhere close. Some out in the channel of course and some out fishing further out, but nothing I noticed within several hundred yards."

"Did you know Professor Munson personally?"

"Not really. I mean, I knew who he was. We ran into each other in faculty meetings and the faculty section of the dining hall. We served on one of the faculty committees advising the student government. But the math department and the theatre and speech department really don't have much to do with each other. And him not having a wife or kids, there just wasn't much occasion to socialize. We did go to the plays he directed sometimes, especially the musicals. He seemed to know his subject, best I could tell."

"Who did he socialize with?"

"Nobody, as far as I know. He had to teach a full load, plus direct two plays a semester, including a Shakespeare and a musical once each year. They rehearse at night, after classes, so I think he spent almost all his time dealing with that. His theatre students probably knew him better than anybody on the faculty. I did sign a sympathy card we passed around after his mother died last month, but that was about all the personal stuff between us."

"You didn't hear any rumors about him?"

"You mean that he was queer? I heard that, but I didn't believe it. This is a very conservative college. It's a closed campus, students have to go to chapel every week, women have to wear dresses to class, men coat and tie. This would be a really lousy place to be if you're queer. And we certainly never got any complaints from the theatre students about him coming on to anybody, male or female. Strictly professional, as far as I knew. Nobody on the faculty ever said anything more than he was a little old to be unmarried. I knew what they were getting at, but I don't believe in leaping to those kinds of conclusions. If my boys had started hanging around with him it might have been different, but we just never had that much to do with him that I could make up my mind."

"You know if he fished much?"

"Oh, I'd see him out on the pier with a pole sometimes, mostly like this time, during a holiday when he didn't have classes or rehearsals. I think I heard he was from some little town on the Outer Banks of North Carolina, where I guess everybody fishes some."

"Any idea what happened to his fishing stuff?"

"Security guard took it. No idea what they did with it. Is there some problem?"

"Just following procedure. I have to write a report for the files and everything, just in case."

"Well, as far as I know, he didn't have any money besides what the college paid. And if he did have any enemies, they would have been out of town for the holidays."

"Any idea why he was here?"

"Just a guess, but he had to go home for a week last month for his mother's funeral. Probably didn't have any money left after paying for the funeral and all."

"What did she die of?"

"Cancer of some kind, I heard. Really not sure."

There was a pause in the conversation.

"Is there anything else, Officer?"

"You like teaching here, Mr. Covington?"

"It's OK. Better than high school. My wife likes it because she doesn't have to cook most of the time. She teaches in a public school in town, and it's hard to teach and keep house at the same time."

"I bet. I may need to talk to your boys, but I think that's it for right now. Have to see what else I find."

"I would appreciate if that could be avoided. They're already asking questions about death and dying."

"I'm sure. I'll try to avoid it if I can."

"Thanks. Well, you know how to find me."

"Thank you for your cooperation."

And W. T. Covington turned and walked back to his converted warehouse duplex apartment. Carlos Ruffin stood there for a few more minutes, then got in his car and drove to the security office by the main gate. There, he asked to see the items that had been collected from the pier after the body had been taken away. There was a canvas camp stool, a small rod and reel, and a tackle box with several types of hooks and sinkers. They said the bait had been tossed into the river. No mention was made of the portable radio, nor was it with the other items. Carlos did not bring it up but made a note in his file.

He then asked for access to the deceased's apartment and followed an officer's car to the place Hough had pointed out. The officer unlocked the padlock, went in with him, but just sat on the sofa, the only seat in the living room, while Carlos conducted his search. There was a little Christmas tree on the coffee table, but it only had three decorative balls, no lights or tinsel. That was the only holiday decoration. No wrapping paper in the trashcans. There was a small TV and a regular radio set, but no pictures on the walls. Everything was the basic white paint of all apartments.

He moved on to the kitchen, looking in the fridge, cabinets, and drawers. There was a box of Rice Krispies, a box of 5-Minute Oatmeal, a carton of milk, a container of pimento cheese, and a loaf of Wonder Bread. A couple of plastic plates and saucers, some utensils, and a few mugs and glasses were all there was in the cabinets and drawers. Evidently, Munson, like most of the faculty, had taken most of his meals in the dining hall.

The master bedroom had a double bed, neatly made up with plain white sheets and a beige comforter. The clothes in the dresser and closet all seemed the normal kind of thing a drama teacher at a conservative college would have worn. Carlos looked for hiding places that might have had erotica of some kind, but there wasn't even a Playboy magazine, not to mention whatever the homosexual equivalent was, if there was one.

One of the other bedrooms was completely empty of furniture but had a few cardboard boxes. Carlos looked in the open boxes and saw what looked like the personal items of an old woman, mostly clothes, knick-knacks, and some diabetic equipment, along with a few old pictures of a man in an army uniform and of a young boy at various ages, sometimes with a woman who looked like she was his mother. Carlos added the pictures and a few of the other items to his file.

The third bedroom had been converted into a home office with a desk, bookcase, and a drafting table. The drafting table held what looked like the technical drawings for some theatre set. Carlos couldn't identify the play for sure but thought it might be "J. B." by Archibald MacLeish, with its distinctive circus ring setting. It had been a hit on Broadway about five years before. Carlos had seen the local community theatre production last year and had helped build the set. The bookcase had an entire shelf of French and Dramatist Play Service acting editions of plays. Some of them had scribbles in the margins as if they had been used by Munson while acting a role in a production. He evidently had not played leading roles, just character parts and supporting roles. The other shelves had theatre textbooks and collections of classic plays, including the complete works of William Shakespeare and other playwrights Carlos was familiar with. There was a typewriter on the desk, but nothing except for what looked like notes for lesson plans and class presentations in any of the drawers or notebooks scattered across the top. Only in the bottom drawer did he find anything personal, a stack of letters addressed to Munson.

Carlos took out the top few letters. They were all from the same address, a rural post office in Duck, North Carolina. Carlos knew it was a little town on the Outer Banks, north of Kitty Hawk and the other tourist areas. Opening the top letter, he read,

Dear Son,

The doctor says the cancer is back, worse than ever. Combined with the diabetes and the high blood pressure, there isn't any hope. I might see Christmas, but probably not. I'll try to make it that long and hope you can come for

the holidays. If I don't get to write again, just remember that I loved you and tried to do right by you, especially after the war. We had some hard times, but you were a good boy and have turned into a fine man. It's hard to believe you are really teaching in a college, going through what you had to go through. I'm very proud of you. I'm sorry I can't leave you anything but debts and a broken-down house with the mortgage still not paid off. I don't need a fancy funeral. Sorry to leave you alone like this. Remember me as fondly as you can.

Mom.

Carlos put the letter back in the envelope, then put the entire stack of letters in with the other papers in his file. Then he noticed a box that had been behind the letters. He opened it to reveal a Purple Heart medal and a death notice from the army. "Pvt. Chester Lee Munson was killed in action on December 26, 1944, near the town of Bastogne, Belgium." Carlos recognized the date and location. This was the Battle of the Bulge. Carlos's father had been a tank driver in the battalions that had rushed to relieve Bastogne, but not in time to save Chester Lee Munson. A quick calculation in his head told Carlos Elmer Munson would have been twelve years old when his father died. He added the box and its contents to the pile of things he was collecting as evidence and for the next of kin.

After that, he found no more personal items, even after a careful search for secret drawers in the desk or elsewhere. There was nothing unusual in the bathroom, no medicines in the medicine cabinet stronger than aspirin. Finally, he collected the campus security officer from his nap on the sofa. The officer didn't even ask what Carlos was taking from the apartment. He simply locked up behind them and asked if Carlos needed anything else. Carlos said he needed to see Munson's office on the other side of campus. The officer got in his car and led him to a building full of nothing but professors' offices and classrooms.

The officer let him into the very small office that had nothing but a small desk and a couple of chairs for students who came for help. It took no time to determine there was nothing here except textbooks, lesson plans, grade books, and a Rolodex of phone numbers for the other faculty. Nothing worth taking as evidence. Carlos put what little he had collected in the trunk of his car, sat inside out of the wind for a few minutes, then drove out through the main gate and back to the police precinct building.

Once back at his desk, he began typing a report to the coroner. "Preliminary investigations suggest Elmer Munson may have died of a self-administered injection of insulin while sitting alone on a pier on the James River. This may be difficult to prove because the syringe and insulin bottle are probably floating down the James into Hampton Roads. If it is possible, please test the body for evidence of the presence of insulin in very high doses, especially in a man who did not have diabetes. He probably acquired the insulin and syringe from his mother's estate after her recent death. Motive for suicide is suggested by other evidence, but this alone would be inconclusive without some laboratory confirmation. I am informed by the college that they are still trying to identify the next of kin, so I will contact the authorities in Duck, NC, to help in that effort."

Carlos put the carbon copies in the file folder and the other items in an evidence box. He put the preliminary report in an express inter-office mail envelope, sealed it, and walked it to the "Out-going to Coroner" box. He then walked out to the parking lot and sat in his car for twenty minutes before going back inside.

Yuma Mystery

Detective Captain Cathy Higuera stood in front of the grating of strap iron that formed the door of the cell in the Yuma Territorial Prison. She was using her flashlight to peer into the shadows between the outer and inner doors of the prison cell. Lying on the ground, there was the very naked, very dead body of a very large Caucasian man. Best she could tell from outside the iron door, he had been shot several times, stabbed many more, and his genitals had been cut off and stuffed into his mouth. She wasn't sure in which order things had gone but hoped the genital mutilation had been after he was dead.

Of course, the Yuma Territorial Prison wasn't a prison anymore. It had been back in the last years of the 1800s and early years of the 1900s, then had become a school, of all things, for a few years. The mascot of Yuma High School was still the "Criminal." Now, it was a state historic park and one of the main tourist attractions in the area. Built on a hill overlooking what was left of the Colorado River after all the farms and cities up-river took all the water they could, with California visible across the river and Mexico just a little south and west, the prison had been a less than pleasant residence for various famous and lesser-known villains and lawbreakers of the Old West.

Now, Captain Higuera stood in the sun in the courtyard between the two rows of cells, seeing what she could while waiting for the park ranger to arrive with the key to the padlock holding the iron door shut. It was August, not yet nine o'clock in the morning, and already in the eighties, headed up well above one hundred degrees by the afternoon. Yuma had a wonderful climate, lots of sunny, clear days and cool nights, but August was not its best season for outdoor activities, even with the ultra-low humidity. At least not during the afternoon. Picnics at midnight in the dunes just across the river could be magical.

Higuera had grown up in Yuma. You just had to know how to handle the heat. She wore a white, cotton, long-sleeve shirt and light khaki pants that covered most of her skin, protecting it from the sun. Her brown skin boasted her Hispanic heritage and helped protect her from the solar rays. Her badge was prominently displayed in a badge holder hung around her neck, resting just below her cleavage. August in Yuma was no time to be wearing a jacket during the day, so her police-issued .45 automatic was on full display in its shoulder holster. Her hat was a Stetson, custom fit, given to her by the mounted patrol officers, with the Yuma Police Department logo on the front. Its brim shaded the back of her neck; covered her bobbed, black hair, and kept her eyes in shadow most of the time.

She was short, barely meeting the minimum height requirements of the department, and maybe having to fudge that a quarter of an inch. She was also slim, with not much body fat anywhere. This made her look unimposing and not much of a threat. She had used that mild appearance to defuse many situations as a uniformed officer. But it had also caused some people to underestimate her. Most of them had lived to regret that. A couple had not lived. Now approaching the age of fifty, she was the captain of the detectives and nobody on the Yuma police force thought anybody deserved it more.

So when the park volunteer now standing a few feet behind her had found the body locked in the cell while checking the grounds before the park opened, and Detective Livingston, a newly promoted detective who was also standing a few feet behind her, had arrived and seen what the situation was, Livingston had not hesitated to call the boss detective. So, here she was, staring at a young man's naked body in a very old, very locked prison cell.

She heard a noise and turned to see a crowd approaching; the park ranger with the key, the police photographer, two police crime scene techs, the assistant coroner, and the assistant coroner's assistant. She held up a hand to stop them. She checked to see if she was leaving any footprints. Most of the narrow outdoor courtyard was hard-packed dirt, but the area right in front of the cell doors was concrete. The buildings created a little wind tunnel effect that kept the dirt and dust stirred up, so nothing resembling a footprint was visible.

She called the assistant coroner forward and played her light over the body.

"You agree he's dead?"

"Hell yeah."

"OK, then let the photog and the lab techs have the first go."

"No problem."

The assistant coroner went back to the back of the line where the stretcher was waiting. Cathy called the photographer and lab techs forward.

"I doubt footprints out here are a possibility, but there may be some inside. Right now, check the bars for fingerprints and DNA before we open them. Paul, lots of pictures of that door and the area around it. After we open the door I'll want the body, the ground, the walls, and the second door inside, then inside the cell. And later, I want pictures of whatever is on the roof."

"You got it, boss."

Cathy stepped back and let the specialists do their thing. She took the opportunity to text her husband. *Murder case. May be late. Get pizza.* Her husband, Robert Delarm, (she had kept her maiden name on the job) was a teacher at Yuma High School (English and journalism). He was still out of school for the summer and would deal with the kids. Not that they needed much dealing with anymore. They had two children, a boy about to enter his senior year at high school and a girl entering her sophomore year. Cathy and Robert married when Robert was fresh out of his master's program and just starting to teach and she was finishing up her undergrad work at the University of

Arizona. They had deliberately chosen to live outside the catchment area of Yuma High so they would not live near the students her husband was teaching. Her kids now were enrolled at the other high school in town, her alma mater, Kofa High, named after the King of Arizona gold mine that had been outside town. The kids never had to be in the same school as their father, which was good for all of them.

As she waited, another person ambled up. Dan Ochoa was the local rep of the Criminal Investigations Division of the Arizona Department of Public Safety. Now in his forties, toting a beer belly above his belt, he still showed the scars of childhood acne and a couple of fights. He handed her a cold bottle of water and passed another to Livingston. Cathy swigged a third of it before removing it from her lips. Another secret of living in the desert; drink lots of water.

"Hello, Ochoa. Thanks. You here to take jurisdiction since this is a state park?"

"Boss in Phoenix says as long as it's you on the case and you want it, I'm just here to aid and assist."

"Sounds good."

"You want to fill me in."

"Park volunteer over there was doing her regular check of the grounds before opening to the tourists. Saw the body in the cell behind the locked door. This isn't one of the cells they open for the tourists, so she didn't have a key. Called 911, reported a murder. Detective Livingston here arrived first, decided this was not run of the mill, and called me. Park Ranger arrived and went to look for the key. It's kept locked in a safe in the main office."

"Any idea who the victim is?"

"Not yet. Shouldn't be too hard to find out. He's huge, at least six feet eight, probably around 250 pounds, best I can tell. Been repeatedly shot, stabbed, and had his manhood rammed between his jaws. Not sure which order yet."

"Ouch."

"Yeah."

"Only one key?"

"That's what the park ranger says."

"So the big question is how did he get in."

"Well, the first question anyway. But one question at a time."

At that point, one of the lab techs called her over.

"This whole place has been wiped clean as a whistle. Probably a rag with bleach. We're getting nothing. You want to let us inside?"

"In a minute."

Cathy began to examine the door itself. There were a few scratches around the two hinges, and it didn't seem to be quite exactly beneath the half-circle grid of strap iron that filled the space between the top of the door and the arch of the doorway. She compared that with the doors to the cells on either side. She grabbed the door and lifted. It was heavy, but she had been known to lift a few weights in her day. Instead of hitting the grid above, it grated against it and moved up. An inch was all that was needed to pull it clear of the hinges. She pulled it outward and it pivoted on the ring implanted in the wall that held the padlock. Not far, but maybe enough away from the hinged wall that even a person as big as the deceased could squeeze through.

Cathy tried to put it back in place, but had to rest the bottom of the door on the ground for a second. Livingston and a lab tech stepped forward to help her, but she shook her head and they backed off. Regripping the door for better leverage, she tried again to lift the door back into place so the shortened hinge pins would slide back into place. It took three tries, but she managed to do it. Once again the door was closed and locked, with the padlock still locked and in place. Livingston turned to Dan Ochoa.

"And that's why she's the captain."

Cathy signaled to the ranger to bring the key but asked to see it before it was used. It was a very old key, the large, iron kind from around the turn of the previous century. But the notches and protrusions showed it was not some standard skeleton key.

"Was it right where it should have been?"

"We keep the keys to the cells that aren't opened for the tourists in a locked box in a safe, in my office, which is behind a locked door, in a locked building. I had to use my keys and a memorized combination to get in. Nothing had been jimmied."

"This is the only key?"

"As far as I know. These padlocks and keys are all very old, around a hundred years. I guess a good locksmith could pick one in ten seconds, but nobody has used this key in weeks. Just when we fumigate the cells for spiders. Otherwise, it stays exactly where I found it today."

"Any security cameras?"

"At the main gate, office, museum, and gift shop, sure. But not out here. It's adobe, strap iron, and empty cells. Why bother?"

"OK, but to be sure . . ."

"I'll send you the recordings we have."

"Thank you. I'll also need a list of all your employees and volunteers. Anybody else have access to the park at night?"

"Well, several people have keys. I'll mark who on the list. Otherwise, there's fences and walls, so it would be hard to sneak in after dark, even if you knew the grounds. But there are a couple of places, maybe. With ladders or something. I mean, it is a prison, after all. I'll look around and see if I see anything."

She signaled him to unlock the cell. Even with the key, it took a minute to get the padlock to cooperate. Once it was out of the ring in the wall, the techs moved in to remove the door entirely and get to the hinge pins that had been cut.

"I need to know how they were cut and how long ago."

"Yes, Captain. We'll do what we can."

With the door now out of the way, Cathy and Livingston moved up and knelt just outside the door, shining their flashlights into the shadows.

"More bleeding around the gunshot wounds. Not much in the stab wounds. Big knife though."

"So, he was shot first, stabbed later."

"Coroner will tell us for sure."

Cathy held her light on the male organ in the mouth. Even in death, it was impressive in size.

"I could think of a lot better things to do with that."

Livingston glanced at the captain, but her face betrayed no smile.

"So, what do you think it means?"

"Well, I'd say it means sex comes into this somewhere."

"Revenge for rape? Jealous boyfriend lost his girl to this guy?"

"Heaven knows."

"Well, you just showed a female could have closed that door. And a female would be able to get him to take his clothes off. Some kinky sex in a cell, then *pow, pow*?"

"Let's find out who this guy is before we jump to any conclusions. Might not be a girl involved even. Get a close-up of the face and send it to the basketball coach out at Western Arizona College, see if he recognizes him. Can't exactly search his pockets for ID."

"OK."

Livingston leaned in long enough to take a picture with a cellphone. They then stepped back and let the photographer and lab techs in. The coroner's assistant was just behind them, inserting a thermometer into the liver. Cathy walked back over to Ochoa and drank the last of her water. Livingston stayed busy making calls and sending texts. They stood in silence, watching the technical people efficiently examine everything. After a few minutes, Livingston came back to them.

"His name was William Robert Able. Twenty years old from Gila Bend. He was the second-string center on the Arizona Western basketball team. Lived on campus. He was taking summer courses to get his academic eligibility back for his second year. Coach said he was tall and strong but kept tripping over his own feet. Not a quick learner on the court either, according to the coach. Still, he's not happy about having to recruit a replacement at this late date. He will email what info they have about next of kin and contact information and keep this under his hat until we tell him he can notify people. I don't think he wants to be the one to call the parents first."

"I don't think anybody does, but I guess I will as soon as we get confirmation. Tell the coroner's people where to start looking for matches to the fingerprints."

"Right."

Just then the park ranger reappeared and handed Cathy a few pieces of paper.

"I printed out a list of our employees and their addresses and phone numbers, and another list of volunteers with just phone numbers. It's a good bit longer since some people only volunteer a few hours a week."

"Any of these people associated with Arizona Western College in any way?"

"Well, let's see. Among the employees, I think Jane Fram takes art classes out there sometimes. She's a pretty good artist. Can't think of anybody else among the employees. Among the volunteers, Robyn Dinwiddie works out there, a librarian or something. Carol Olin used to be a student, but I think she finished a year or two ago. Tom Miller used to be a maintenance man there until he retired. Donnalyn Frazier has taken a class or two, I think, but at the extension in town, not the main campus. Peggy Novakovich maybe, I'm not sure. She just works a couple of hours a week in the gift shop, doesn't do tours. Maybe some others I don't know about. There are a lot of them, and I don't know everybody that well."

"And who has keys?"

"I put a little check by the names. It's all four rangers; I'm Bob Kelly, then Debbie Gilmore, Dean Pooler, and Kathleen Winebarger. Also, Genie Berndt, who runs the gift shop, and Jane Fram, who's the museum curator." At least that's all I know about.

"OK, thanks."

"I'll go look for breaches in the walls or fences now."

"Good. Let me know."

"For sure."

The assistant coroner approached, holding a thermometer.

"Liver temp says eight to twelve hours ago, assuming a low of around seventy degrees last night."

"So sometime around ten and two o'clock last night."

"Best guess, very preliminary. You know the drill."

"Oh, yeah."

"Can't say for sure but looks like three shots to the heart were first; other shots and stabbings, and the other stuff, were after he was on the ground. We'll check fingernails for skin scrapings and the, you know, for vaginal secretions, but don't hold your breath on those."

"I know. Just do what you can."

"Right."

"You said three shots, all in the heart?"

"Yeah, real close together. Close range, a foot or two, but still good shooting."

"None of those three came later, after he was down?"

"Looks like *pop, pop, pop,* pause, fall, then *pop, pop, pop* to the lower guts. But let me get him on the table to be sure."

"Caliber?"

"I'll have to dig them out, but based on the size of the holes, I'd guess .38. Can I have the body now?"

"If the techs are done with it."

"They want it out of their way."

"OK then."

"I'll confirm ID as soon as I can run the fingerprints."

"Call me."

"Count on it."

The assistant coroner waved the stretcher forward and they began the process of moving the body back to the coroner's lab in the Yuma Regional Medical Center. Dan stepped forward.

"I've got a contact in Gila Bend, if you want me to expedite those fingerprints."

"Please."

He took out his phone and went over to talk to the assistant coroner.

Cathy handed the lists of names to Livingston.

"Photo of this to me, Ochoa, and back to the office. The ones the ranger mentioned; Fram, Dinwiddie, Olin, Miller, Frazier, and Novakovich, see if any of them have a record, and try to find out how old they are, look them up on Facebook or whatever."

"Right."

Livingston pulled out his phone again and stepped away to a quieter spot. Cathy moved into the shade. Dan came back to her.

"They'll work it out."

"Yeah. How's Ann and the kids?"

"Good, good. I'll be glad when school starts again. I love my children—all three of them—but small doses are easier to take."

"They'll be off to college before you know it."

"Yours, maybe. My oldest is still in middle school. We got a late start. I robbed the cradle marrying Ann, so we waited a few years for her to finish college and everything."

"Still, time flies by."

"Don't I know it."

They stood in the shade for a while, watching the others work. The volunteer who had found the body came over to them.

"Do you need me anymore?"

"Did Detective Livingston get all your contact information?"

"Name, address, phone, email, everything."

"We still need you to sign a formal statement. Just saying what you saw and what you did between the time you arrived here this morning and when I got here."

"I could go back to the office and type that up right now."

"OK, but either I or Detective Livingston will have to review it and witness the signature."

"No problem. Be back in a little while."

She walked back toward the office. Just then the ranger came back.

"I walked the entire perimeter with one of the other rangers. We can't find any sign of anybody sneaking in. Can we let the tourists in once the body is removed? There's getting to be a line out front."

"Ask one of the uniformed officers to bring some crime scene tape and tape off the area in front of the cell. I'll have somebody stand guard probably the rest of the day."

"Fine with me. I'll bring them a chair and a cooler of water."

"Good. Thanks."

Cathy pulled out her cell phone and sent a text arranging for the officer to watch the crime scene, then started responding to emails and doing other electronic paperwork that comes with being a captain. Dan did the same, and soon the three detectives were lined up in the shade like teenagers with cell phones, doing everything except talking to each other. Eventually, the volunteer came back with her typed-up statement. Cathy reviewed it and saw it was a very good summary of what the volunteer had seen and done that morning. She had her date and sign it, then she and Dan signed as witnesses. Cathy then took a picture with her cell phone camera and sent it to Livingston, Ochoa, and to her office email. She then folded up the original and put it in her pocket.

By then, the body had been carted away, the area around the cell was taped off, and a uniformed officer was on duty. Crowds of tourists were wandering by, intrigued by the combination of ancient and modern crime. Soon, the crime scene techs and the photographer signaled that they had done what they could and would be leaving as soon as they collected their equipment. They basically reported not finding much of anything, but promised to run what lab tests they could as soon as possible.

Dan Ochoa glanced at this watch.

"It's almost noon. Even detectives have to eat. Can I talk you into meeting at Lutes and regrouping over their *Especiál*?"

"Ochoa, you eat too much junk."

"And I enjoy every bite of it. You can have one of their lettuce wedges or something. I know it costs more than Eduardo's, but if you go back to the office you'll just end up at Jack-in-the-Box across the road."

"What do you think, Livingston? You up for Lutes?"

"After this morning, I see the virtues of living for today. Sure."

"OK, Lutes it is. See you there."

Cathy stopped by the park office to tell the ranger that they were leaving except for the uniform guarding the taped-off area, at least until the techs said they didn't need to follow up on anything. Hence, she was last to arrive at Lutes Casino Restaurant a couple of blocks away on the other side of I-8. It wasn't a casino anymore, just a bar and restaurant with pool tables and pinball machines and lots of kitschy movie posters and other fake Western memorabilia as decoration. Ochoa and Livingston had gotten a table in the back but were waiting for Cathy before ordering.

Ochoa did indeed order the *"Especiál,"* which was a combination cheeseburger and hot dog on the same bun with lots of toppings and hot sauce. He also sprang for a large basket of fries to share. Livingston was a little more millennial, opting for the quinoa burger. Cathy considered the lettuce wedge, but splurged on the chicken taco salad, not being sure when she would get to the pizza at home if her kids left her any. They had all ordered iced tea, and obeyed the desert rule to drink as much liquid as you can, while you can.

As they were eating, Cathy got a text from the coroner.

"Coroner's office confirms deceased as William Robert Able. Gila Bend had his prints in their files due to a couple of drunk and disorderlys. You have the next of kin info?"

"Forwarding it to you right now."

"I'll be back in a few minutes."

She got up and left the restaurant, walking out to the fountain in the plaza to get a private place for the phone call. Entering the contact number for the parents that Livingston had sent her, she listened to the phone ring.

"Hello."

"Is this Louisa Able?"

"Yes."

"Mrs. Able, I'm Captain Higuera of the Yuma Police Department."

"Yes?"

"I'm very sorry to have to tell you that your son William Able has been killed."

"What?"

"Your son William is dead. I'm sorry."

"Is this some kind of bad joke? If it is, I'm going to whale the living daylights out of somebody."

"No, ma'am. I'm sorry. If you want to hang up and call the Yuma Police Department and ask for Captain Higuera for a death notification, they will transfer you back to me."

"My god, what happened? Was it a car accident?"

"No, ma'am, he was shot."

"Shot? How? Who?"

"That's what we're investigating now. Do you have any idea who might have shot your son?"

"No. Good, god. Most of his friends were gone for the summer. He had to stay for summer school, but he hardly knew anybody else who had to."

"Was he dating anybody? Another student or somebody who lived in Yuma?"

"Well, I'm sure he was dating some girl. More likely girls. You know, sports star, handsome, and, you know, tall. Girls tend to like men like that. He was just a big teddy bear."

"Did he ever get into any trouble?"

"You mean knocking girls up? No, not that I know of. I guess it's possible, but most girls these days, you know, take precautions."

"What about other kinds of trouble, drinking, drugs, anything?"

"No drugs. Basketball was too important to him. He didn't drink much except a couple of times. If he drank too much, he sort of got a little wild. He was young, you know. But he never hurt anybody or anything. And no stealing or anything. We raised him better than that."

"I'm sure you did, ma'am."

"Oh god, I've got to call his father."

"Please."

"Then what do we do? Captain, what do we do? Do we have to come to Yuma immediately?"

"You'll need to come to Yuma, but it doesn't have to be right away. We can't release the body until after the autopsy. You could call a funeral home in Gila Bend if you have one you are familiar with and ask them to arrange a transfer back to Gila Bend. They would have contacts here that could handle it. You would probably have to pick up William's possessions from the college in person and deal with any payments or refunds, but again, that's not for today. Do you have a pastor or somebody who could walk you through this?"

"Maybe my husband knows someone."

"OK, good. I will need you to be available in case I have further questions or need to reach you for some reason. Is this the best phone number for you?"

"Yes, yes."

"Good. I really am very sorry, Mrs. Able. I have children, so I can imagine how . . . well, I'm just very sorry."

"Thank you."

"I'll let you know what we find out about who did this to your son."

"Thank you."

"Goodbye."

"Goodbye, Captain."

Cathy ended the call and stared into the fountain for a minute before going back into Lutes. Ochoa was eating a brownie sundae and Livingston was taking the last bite of an ice cream cone. She sat down to finish her taco salad.

"How did it go?" asked Livingston.

"His mother said he was a big teddy bear unless he was drinking, then he got a little wild. He was popular among the females, but she didn't know any specifics. I doubt she knew the half of it."

"While you were outside I finished looking up the people on the list who had some contact with Arizona Western."

"And?"

"OK, Jane Fram is the museum curator, fifties, historian, undergrad degree in history from ASU, no record, hobby is painting desert landscapes. Takes art classes at the college on a regular basis. Two kids grown and moved out, husband is a lawyer, mostly real estate law. She's the only one with both Arizona Western connections and a key to the prison.

"Tom Miller isn't on Facebook, but he has a record with us for two DUIs. He's about seventy, retired for the past two years according to the college.

"Robyn Dinwiddie is the Assistant Librarian at the college. Forties, divorced, no kids. Gives tours at the prison on Sundays, so she would have been there the day before the murder. It's not explicit, but I get the impression from her Facebook page that perhaps she might prefer other women to men, though she can't be too open about it, even these days. Just an impression on my part, though. No record.

"Donnalyn Frazier is in her thirties, takes classes in Spanish at the downtown center. Never any classes at the main campus as far as the college records go. Married, husband is a doctor, one kid who just started school. Couple of parking tickets.

"Carol Olin is only in her twenties. Single, but just an associate degree from the college, a year ago. Waitress at Golden Corral. No record as far as I can find.

"Peggy Novakovich is the youngest, the right age to be in college, but evidently decided it wasn't for her after a couple of classes. Her parents own the truck stop on I-8 just outside of town, and evidently, she's taking a gap year or two before finding herself. No record though."

"OK, good. Go by the coroner's office and pick up a death certificate and whatever other documentation they'll give you, then beat it out to Arizona Western and search Able's dorm room and locker in the gym. Grab any computer, cellphone, diary, roster of other players there this summer, record of practices or other team activities, anything that would tell us who he had been dealing with and what he had been doing the past few weeks. If there's no roommate, seal the room until the parents can get there. If there is, see what the school can do to protect his stuff until it can be picked up. And tell the coach he can tell other people now. And find out if he knows anything about Able's social life."

"Right."

"Ochoa, you want to aid and assist by splitting the list of people with college connections? Need to know where they were last night and if they knew William Able."

"Sure. Did he go by Bill? Anybody know?"

"Bill Able? Sounds like a bad lawyer. I sure hope not."

"Just curious."

"I'll take Fram since she also has a key and the two young ones, Olin and Novakovich."

"So I get the old man, Miller, the maybe lesbian, Dinwiddie, and the doctor's wife with the little kid, Frazier."

"Ann can send me a thank you note later."

"Very funny."

"Everybody text the other two if you find anything hot."

"You want dessert? We can wait."

"We crack this, you can buy me a slushie."

"Deal."

They paid their bills and left on their separate tasks. Cathy played a hunch and went back to the prison. It had several tourists braving the afternoon heat but was basically quiet. She flashed her badge at the gate and went to the prison museum. Sure enough, Jane Fram was there, talking to the volunteer docent on duty. Cathy identified herself and asked to talk in private. Jane Fram was in her fifties, hair just starting to go gray and pulled back in a bun. She looked a little physically past her prime, like the kind of woman who would be the curator of a little museum but was dressed in a colorful smock more befitting the artist she tried to be. She took Cathy back to her office and closed the door.

"Before you ask, I still have my key to the gate. It's on the ring with my office key, separate from my house and car keys. It never left my purse."

"And last night you were . . . ?"

"At home, in bed with my husband. He's a lawyer. He told me you'd have to ask."

"And did you know William Able?"

"I saw him in the art classrooms a couple of times, out at Arizona Western. I take a painting class out there once in a while. Just trying to improve. I think he was taking a beginning art for dummies class or art appreciation or something, probably trying to help his GPA. He's kind of hard to miss, or was, anyway. I never talked to him."

"You hear anything about him, who he was talking to?"

"There was a joke that some of the female art majors were offering to "model" for him, if you know what I mean. But the comeback was that we had it backward, they wanted him to model for them. He was an impressive physical specimen, though evidently not as athletic as he looked. If he was really good, he wouldn't have been at Arizona Western."

"It could have been just poor grades."

"Possibly. I don't follow athletics that much. Never went to the games or anything."

"Any idea how he got in last night? Or opened the cell?"

"None. You know, detective, I could have answered these questions on the phone."

"I find body language tells me a lot. Especially if people don't have time to prepare for questioning."

"So, what's my body language telling you?"

"That you're annoyed with me, and a little nervous, but probably not enough to lie. The nervous part is natural. The question is, why are you annoyed? Your husband told you it would be standard procedure to track down the keys."

"Margaret Seager, the volunteer who found the body, told me what happened to him. That anybody could think I might have anything to do with that is offensive."

"Not as offensive as actually doing that to a man. Thank you for your cooperation, Mrs. Fram."

And she turned and left. Carol Olin was next on the list, so she drove down I-8 to the Sixteenth Street exit and went into town a couple of blocks. She asked to see the manager of the all-you-can-eat buffet restaurant, told him she needed to see Carol Olin, and he pointed her out and told Cathy she could use the empty room reserved for private groups. It was glassed in but should be quieter than the rest of the place, even though it was past the lunch rush. Cathy flashed her badge and identified herself, then escorted Carol to the quiet room where they could sit across a table from each other.

Carol was dressed in her waitress uniform, which said nothing about her personality. But it did reveal a slight figure much like Cathy's, only a few inches taller. Her dark brown hair was parted in the middle and fell straight to her shoulders, but was pinned behind her ears. Basically, she looked tired, the long-lasting kind of tired that a couple of days off could not even dent, too tired to be only in her twenties.

"Is this about my parents?"

"No. Were you expecting something about your parents?"

"My father has early dementia. He's wandered off a couple of times."

"No, nothing like that."

"Good."

"I just need to know where you were last night between ten and two o'clock."

"Why?"

"Answer the question first, please."

"Well, officially I got off work at nine, but it was probably nine thirty before I actually pulled out of the parking lot. I went straight home and went to bed."

"Alone?"

"I was in bed alone, if that's what you're asking, but my mother, father, and brother all saw me come in and saw me there in the morning for breakfast."

"And you are a student at Arizona Western?"

"I was until May a year ago. I finished my associate's degree, finally. Took forever."

"You had problems?"

"I started at U of A, fresh out of high school at Kofa High. But toward the end of my freshman year, my mother had her second heart attack. Then my dad started showing signs of dementia. I came home for the summer, and things just sort of fell apart. My dad had to take early retirement for disability; my mother couldn't even do some of the housework, not to mention hold a job. My brother tried to help, but he was still in high school then. The health insurance didn't come close to covering everything. Let's just say I never made it back to Tucson. I switched to part-time at the community college here. Got this job. It doesn't pay a lot, but the tips help, and Peter Seitz, the manager, is flexible with my schedule. I used to date his son in high school, and even though his son went off to ASU and I went to U of A and that was the end of that, I think Peter still likes me. He'd work my hours around my classes if he could. And I get to work a split shift so I have a couple of hours in the middle of the day to gulp down the free lunch and get home for an hour to check on my parents."

"I'll try not to make you miss your break. You volunteer at Yuma Territorial Prison?"

"Now that I don't have classes. One or two afternoons a week. On my days off. I give the afternoon tours that nobody else wants because it's hot. Gets me out of the house. I love my dad, but I have to get out of the house on a regular basis. It's just too much, seeing him fading away like that."

"It must be hard."

"You have no idea. He used to be so smart, you know?"

"When you were at the college, did you ever meet a young man named William Able?"

"You mean the big oaf who tries to play basketball?"

"I think that's who I'm talking about. Do you know him?"

"Not personally. He started the year after I finished. I heard about him though."

"Heard what?"

"Thinks he's god's gift to women. Plays more than basketball, if you know what I mean."

"I think I get the idea. He plays the field, more than one girl-friend at once."

"Girlfriends, hook-ups, hi and bye. Frankly, I don't know what the women see in him, but he doesn't seem to have trouble getting what he wants. At least from what I hear. My brother is a student there now. And I have a few friends from my student days I keep in touch with. Did he get his hand caught in a cookie jar and somebody called him on it?"

"William Able was shot and killed last night at the Territorial prison."

"Oh god."

"Did any names just pop into your head?"

"Well, I mean, you know . . . Nobody that I think would have shot him. Just, you know, people he might not have treated well. And might not be too sorry he died."

"I really need a lead here. Even just to find out what Able was like. What he was into."

"Or who he was into?"

"Whichever."

"You won't tell them I told you?"

"Not unless I have to. But I need all the help I can get."

"Fannie Franklyn, Roberta Canode, and Nancy Garza. They all had, shall we say, acquaintances with him. They are all students at the college, either full-time or part-time. Fannie was in my American history class, Roberta was in two of my Spanish classes, and Nancy was in my English class. We'd have coffee or something sometimes when we had a break between classes. They were all at the college last year, after I finished, and I heard they all fell under the Able spell at one time or another."

"You have addresses or phone numbers for these people?"

"Fannie lives over on West Twenty-Eighth, near Kofa High. I don't know the street address. Just that she could walk to school. Roberta is on Corona, just a few blocks north of the golf course. I gave her a ride home once. Nancy lives somewhere near Ponderosa Park, I think. I've never been to her house. Hang on a minute."

Carol pulled her cell phone out of her pocket and looked up some phone numbers. Cathy gave her a piece of paper from her little notepad and Carol wrote down names and numbers.

"Thank you. I won't mention you if I can help it. Anything else you can tell me about William Able?"

"According to my brother, he couldn't make a hook shot if his life depended on it."

"Well, I don't think that was what got him killed, but you never know. I'll let you get back to work now. And, Miss Olin . . ."

"Yes?"

"If you do ever need the police for your parents, or whatever, just tell them to tell Captain Higuera."

"Captain Higuera. Got it. Thanks."

"Thank you."

Back in her car, some itch was scratching Cathy's brain. She reviewed her notes from the conversation with Carol, then pulled up on her phone the list of park employees with keys. There it was. Debbie Gilmore, one of the park rangers with a key, lived on Corona Drive. Cathy logged on to her cruiser computer and looked up both Debbie Gilmore and Roberta Canode. Neither one had a criminal record. A little more searching in municipal records showed a John Canode in a house at 1047 Corona Drive, right next door to Jane Gilmore.

Cathy called Livingston.

"Where are you?"

"In the dorm room."

"Have you found his cell phone?"

"No. It's probably with his clothes, along with whatever else he had in his pockets. Wherever all that stuff is."

"What about his laptop?"

"Yeah, I got that, but I'm not in yet. Whatever else this guy was, he wasn't careless about his passwords."

"OK, I've gotten a tip to check out Fannie Franklyn, Roberta Canode, and Nancy Garza. All students at the college. Rumor is they got it on with Able. I'm particularly interested in Roberta Canode; I think she lives next door to Debbie Gilmore, a park ranger with a key."

"That does open up some possibilities. You sure come up with good sources. I can check Facebook and the college records."

"Do that. And fill Ochoa in. I'm skipping Novakovich for now and going out to Gilmore's place."

"OK. Be careful."

"Always."

Cathy called in her destination to the dispatcher, then drove south on Arizona Avenue, entering the subdivision at Robin Lane and winding around toward the back to get to Corona Drive. The subdivision construction looked like hundreds of other houses in Yuma. The houses here were at least fifty years old, if not older. Back then it was probably considered a middle-class subdivision. Now it was more working class, though still way above anything resembling the dire poverty that could be found easily in the area. Over time, the houses had been redecorated and remodeled enough that each one looked a little bit different. But it was cosmetic. They were basically identical in layout. Single-story ranch houses, built on slabs. One-car garages, open living-dining-kitchen spaces, three bedrooms, two baths. Set back from the sidewalk just the length of a car so the driveways could hold a second car if necessary. Front yards were thus very small, mostly natural or rock pebble yards, few with grass that required lots of watering. Houses were about six feet apart, with the ground plan flipped left to right so garages were next to each other on one side and bedroom ends on the other. Backyards were fenced-in with an eight-foot fence for some privacy, but barely room for a small pool before the lot backed into an alley for the trash trucks and separated lots from houses on the other street running parallel. Despite any differences, the houses were all a cheap stucco, basically chicken wire and plaster. It worked well enough in dry climates like Yuma, where rain was a rare event and usually little more than a light shower. That is, if nobody tried to put a fist through the wall from outside. Then a patch job would be required before the next shower to keep the water from soaking into the stucco.

Cathy parked in the street in front of Gilmore's house. Just as she did, a car pulled around her and backed into the driveway. The driver waited for the garage door to go up, then backed into the garage. By then, Cathy was out of her car and walking toward the open garage. The driver got out.

"You looking for me, Officer?"

"Are you Debbie Gilmore? The ranger at Yuma Prison?"

"Guilty."

"I'm Captain Higuera from the Yuma Police. Could we talk for a minute?"

"Could we talk inside? I just did my grocery shopping and I've got ice cream in the car."

"Sure. Could I help you unload?"

"If you don't mind."

"Not at all."

Debbie pulled up the rear door of the SUV and then opened the door in the rear of the garage, which led into the kitchen. Debbie grabbed the first load of grocery bags and Cathy took the rest. They put everything down on the counters in the kitchen, then Debbie went back into the garage to push the button closing the garage door and closed the rear of the SUV. Once back inside, she began unloading the bags and putting frozen stuff in the freezer and chilled food in the refrigerator. Three cats appeared out of nowhere to inspect the groceries and the visitor.

Cathy carefully scratched the ears of the cat examining her footwear.

"In this heat, it starts melting as soon as it leaves the store. If I don't come straight home and put it away, I end up with mush."

"Believe me, I understand."

The pause gave Cathy a chance to look around. Debbie was probably in her late thirties or early forties, still a vigorous-looking woman with a reasonable figure. Being out in the sun as part of her job had given her face a permanent tan and some early aging around the eyes, but her movements said she was energetic and strong. She proclaimed her hanging on to youth with a cut-off shirt tied just below her cleavage, revealing a still taut midriff.

The kitchen was basic, but clean and neat. There was a dining table for eight, but Cathy guessed most meals were eaten at the coffee table in the living room in front of the large-screen TV. The furniture was rustic but comfortable looking. Debbie was not a style maven but had set her house up for her own comfort. There was no sign of a second person living there.

"Is this about the killing at the prison?"

"Yes."

"Well, I don't have an alibi. Sunday and Monday are my days off, and I was here, alone, both days, except when I went shopping or something. But I never met this William Able, and I don't have any connection with the college."

"I was wondering about your keys to the gate."

"Oh, they're here in this drawer."

"Wait! Don't touch them."

Cathy pulled a plastic evidence bag from her pocket and pushed it inside out with her hand. She then opened the indicated drawer in the little table by the door to the garage. Debbie pointed.

"Those."

Cathy picked up a large keyring with at least a dozen keys of various types and sizes on it. She flipped the evidence bag, pulling the keys inside without touching them.

"That's more keys than I was expecting."

"The rangers are the only ones with a full set. Front gate, back gate, ticket booth, cash box, museum, gift shop, office building, maintenance building, storage building, ranger's office, key lockbox, and my drawer in the shared desk. We not only haven't gone high tech, we haven't even coordinated our locks."

"Back gate? I didn't know there was a back gate."

"It's actually not a gate. Not even on the tour. More like an access portal, not even five feet high, one body wide, so prisoners would have to stoop to go in and out. It was used to get to the river for water if the well went dry. A couple of prisoners escaped that way, but their bodies were found later after they drowned trying to cross the river. The Colorado was a bigger river back then, before all the dams and diversions."

"I bet. How many people know about this back gate?"

"It's no big secret. Just something we don't point out to the tourist much."

"So, these keys have been in this drawer all this time?"

"I tossed them in when I got home from work on Saturday, didn't check again until Bob called earlier today to let me know what happened. They're too heavy to carry around in my purse all the time."

"Does anybody else have access to this house?"

"Well, I wasn't home all the time. A couple of my neighbors have keys. I guess they could have come in without me knowing and put them back later. Though I don't think anybody would do that."

"Tell me about these neighbors."

"Well, John Canode next door has a key to this house. He's Mr. Fix-it in the neighborhood. He was over here so often I finally just gave him a key. He or his daughter also comes over to feed my cats sometimes. I travel a lot, hiking, camping, that sort of thing. I was hiking Havasu Canyon just a couple of weeks ago. And I haven't paid for a car mechanic or a repairman in years. I just drop a hint that something isn't working right, and I come home one day and it's fixed. Can't beat a neighbor like that. I also splurge on a maid once a month; she has her own key. But she's never taken anything."

"Tell me about the daughter next door."

"Roberta? Oh, I get it. She's a student at Arizona Western. You think she may have known the victim?"

"You think she did?"

"No idea. She's had a rough go of it, but I don't think she would kill anybody."

"What do you mean by 'rough'?"

"Well, her mother died when she was just a little girl. John did his best, but he raised her more like a boy than a girl. Taught her how to fix things, build stuff. His idea of a toy was a toolset. He was a car mechanic, and a good one, but there was some kind of accident, some very loud noise right in his ears. Nerve damage. He's deaf as a post unless he has his hearing aids turned on, and he turns them off unless he knows somebody is talking to him. Says the background noise is painful.

"He got some money from insurance, but he had to take social security disability when he couldn't hear the engines running anymore. Then, when Roberta was in her junior year at Kofa, he came down with cancer. Used to smoke like a chimney. Chemo and radiation seemed to stop it, but it came back two years ago. He had to go through the torture all over again. He's just a few years older than I am, but he looks eighty, white hair, stooped over, thin as a rail. It's been tough for them both. If it comes back again, I don't think he will take the treatments. Not that they could afford it. Insurance only pays so much. I think they've already run through a second mortgage and a loan against his life insurance. If he dies, Roberta will probably find her inheritance is a debt to pay off. And poor Roberta has pretty much had to take care of herself the past few years, not to mention being his nurse a lot of the time."

"Tell me about her."

"Young, pretty. Hell—sexy. Tall, about five foot ten. Played basketball at Kofa, but didn't even try out at the college. I'm not sure why she even went to college anyway. Academics is not her thing. She would have been better off in a trade school, taking auto mechanics or something. Then she might have a job by now instead of running around."

"I think I better have a talk with Roberta."

"I doubt she's at home. At least, her Jeep isn't there. John probably is though. I'll walk you over."

"That's OK, I can manage."

"I told you, John is deaf as a post. If you don't know how to get his attention, he'll never answer the door."

"OK, but if I tell you to leave, you have to leave right then, OK?"

"You think this is serious?"

"Maybe. Just being careful."

"I may not even wait for your signal to hightail it."

Debbie led the way out the front door and across the few steps to the house next door. Instead of going to the front door, however, she stopped at the garage door and began kicking it, hard. It bore the scars of previous visits.

"John will feel the vibrations if he's in the garage, which he usually is."

After a couple of minutes of pounding, the garage door began to rise. An old Jeep was in the garage, but the hood was up and the engine was hanging in the air on a block and tackle hoist. John Canode stood along the back wall, where there was a workbench with a pegboard across the wall holding dozens of power tools. A mechanic's toolbox on wheels was installed next to the Jeep. Debbie waved at John.

"Debbie, come in. I'll hear you in a minute. Let me get my ears on."

He began to adjust the noticeable hearing aids on the back of both ears. Debbie and Cathy walked to the back of the garage.

"OK, what's up?"

Debbie spoke in a slight yell, "John, this is Captain Higuera from the Yuma Police. We're looking for Roberta."

"Why? What's this about?"

Cathy stepped to take up a position right in front of John. She didn't yell, but looked directly at him and spoke up as clearly as possible.

"Mr. Canode, is Roberta here?"

"No."

"Do you know where she is?"

"Out at the college, I guess. Not sure. She's an adult now; I don't have a tracker on her."

"When did you see her last?"

"Yesterday afternoon. She did grocery shopping for us, really stocked up. Refilled all my prescriptions too. Then she left for dinner with some boy."

"Do you know who?"

"No. Like I said, she's an adult now."

"So you don't know what time she got in last night?"

"No. I turn my ears off at night, can't hear a thing. Sleep like a rock."

"And you didn't see her this morning?"

"I got up late. She was already gone. But she had been here. Her coffee mug was in the dishwasher and a couple of dough-nuts were gone from the box."

"But you didn't see her?"

"No. Are you going to tell me what this is all about?"

"You teach her how to use all these tools?"

"Yeah, sure. I made sure she could take care of herself. She fixes her own car, builds her own furniture. She's good with her hands. When she turned sixteen, I bought her a used Jeep Cherokee. We rebuilt the engine together. She's still driving that thing. Runs like a top."

"Mr. Canode, I think I need to look at Roberta's room."

"Well, I'm not so sure about that . . ."

Debbie intervened.

"John, it's important."

John Canode stood there for a moment, considering. Then he pushed the door into the kitchen open.

"Debbie, you show her."

He turned back to his workbench. His hands shook a little as he picked up a wrench, and he suppressed a cough until the women were through the door. Debbie led the way through the kitchen, down the hall, and to the bedroom in the front corner of the house.

It was a small room. One double-pane sliding window with blinds filled half of the front wall. There was a single bed, a dresser, and a desk. The spot for a laptop on the desk was empty. No adapters for chargers were plugged into the sockets. Atop the dresser were two empty spaces that looked like they used to hold picture frames. Cathy opened the shallow closet trifold doors. Almost half the hangers were empty. There was no sign of any suitcases or backpacks. On the floor where shoes would have been, three spaces were vacant. Cathy went to the dresser and opened the drawers, finding them about half empty. She went to the bathroom in the hall and checked the laundry hamper, which was almost empty. The medicine cabinet had empty space where the birth control pills would have been.

Cathy pulled out her phone and scrolled through her list of contacts, then placed a call.

"*Hola. Capitán Ruiz, por favor. Es Capitán Higuera de Yuma Policía. Gracias.*"

She waited.

"*Armando, es Cathy. Que pasa? Sí, sí, esta bien.* Armando, listen, I need to find out fast if a certain person crossed the border today. *Sí.* Roberta Canode; C-A-N-O-D-E. Caucasian female, early twenties, about five feet, ten inches; probably driving a Jeep Cherokee. *Sí,* I'll wait."

Cathy moved into the living room and signaled Debbie to sit on the sofa. It took about two minutes for Armando to come back on the phone.

"*Sí.* Around nine o'clock. Shopping in San Luis. If she comes back across, hold her for me. We'll get a warrant to you as soon as possible. Murder suspect. *Sí. Sí. Gracias,* Armando. *Tarde.*"

She ended the call and punched up Livingston.

"Livingston? Hang on, I want to conference in Ochoa. Ochoa, you there? Good, I've got both of you. Roberta Canode evidently has done a flyer. She crossed into Mexico about nine this morning at San Luis. If her prints are on Gilmore's ranger keys, we could have a circumstantial case. She reportedly had a relationship with Able that may not have ended well, and her situation at home was less than ideal. Yeah, it's not conclusive, but I think it's enough for a warrant. Livingston, get back to the office and start the paperwork. Ochoa, can you deal with the Sonoran authorities? She's probably headed into the interior, but heaven knows where. Yeah, yeah. No, I have to deal with the father first. He's deaf, has no idea what is going on, and I think he's dying of cancer. This could take a little while. Yeah, see you back at the office."

She hung up just as Debbie approached her.

"You're saying Roberta killed that boy."

"It sure looks that way."

"And ran off to Mexico."

"That's what the Mexican border police are saying."

"What's going to happen to her?"

"I don't know. She seems to have planned all this out. Maybe she has a place to go. I don't know. We will ask the Mexican authorities to look for her, but you know how things are in Mexico these days. She probably has more to worry about from the cartels than the police. Even if we get her back, what we know and what we could prove in court may be different things."

"My God, what is John going to do?"

"I don't think he is going to have much longer."

"No, I guess not."

"It's all so sad. What are you going to tell him?"

"Truth works best in the long run."

"He doesn't have a long run."

"Truth is all I've got."

"Can I be here?"

"Sure."

They went into the garage, where they found John Canode sitting in the driver's seat of the Jeep. He had taken the hearing aids out of his ears and was crying uncontrollably.

At the Baptist Student Union

Kate Dayton strode up to the door of the Baptist Student Union building just off the campus of the University of Arizona in Tucson. The line of police keeping the curious from entering the building parted before her. By now, she was used to people getting out of her way, partly because of the gold badge on her chest and the bits of metal on her collar, partly because she walked like people would get out of her way. She was also used to the stares at her figure as she walked by.

She understood why she was so often described as looking like Dolly Parton, but wondered why all the differences between her and Dolly didn't seem to make much difference. After all, Dolly was only five feet tall, and Kate, at five foot eleven, a full head taller, would tower over her. Also, her hair was both real and black, not to mention worn down and chopped off at her collar. Also, Dolly had that ridiculously small waist that prompted all the jokes about nothing growing in the shade, while Kate, though in fine physical condition, was closer to normal proportions, given her upper measurement. But all the attention was given to how close her bra size was to Dolly's 36DD. But she wasn't quite that big, and, after all, she was a lot taller, so it wasn't such an extreme. But it was definitely the first thing people noticed and, while sometimes useful, enough of a problem that she actually had to make her own uniform and other clothes, long ago realizing that nothing off the rack would ever fit properly. And the last thing she wanted to do was draw attention because something was gaping open somewhere. She drew enough attention as it was.

She entered the glass door and passed by the little lounge on the right with three worn couches and a few other chairs in front of a big screen TV. A door on the left let her glimpse a small room with a plain table and a few chairs around it. Then the hall opened up on the right into a large "all-purpose" room. In the middle of this room was what had caused her to be brought into the case.

In the center of the big room was a ping-pong table, one of the kinds that folds up and then has wheels to be rolled out of the way. On this table lay two completely naked young women, one on top of the other, oriented in opposite directions in the classic "sixty-nine" position so that each one's face was covered by the crotch of the other. There was also a very large sword that had been thrust down through both bodies and then through the wood of the ping-pong table so that the tip of the blade stuck out below. There was a substantial amount of blood and other body fluids on the table and floor. Both women were, to say the least, very dead.

At the moment, the police photographer was working his way around the table, taking pictures from every imaginable angle while the crime scene technicians stood by, waiting impatiently. The medical examiner was also there with an assistant, their tools stacked on the gurney, next in line for access to the body.

Kate took in the scene for a moment, then announced to whoever was listening,

"Well, that's a new one."

She slowly circled the table, being careful to not end up in any of the photographer's pictures. Finally, he lowered his camera, clicked through what he had captured, then nodded to the crime scene techs and stepped back. As the techs swarmed in, Kate crossed to the ME.

"Really weird, huh?" the ME, a woman in her fifties with gray hair and pale skin named Kelsey Smith, asked.

"Yeah, weird. Give me your measuring tape."

The ME assistant popped open one of the cases they carried and handed Kate a metal, retractable, eight-foot measuring tape.

Being careful not to touch anything and not to bump any techs, Cathy took rough measurements of the length of the sword extending below the table, the thickness of the table, the thickness of the two bodies, and then the length of the hilt and pommel and thickness of the guard as they stuck out above the top body. She then returned the tape, made a few notes in a notebook she carried, and took out her phone.

She was strolling through websites when Robert Delahey, the detective who had called her in, walked up.

"Whapping big sword."

"It's a claymore."

"A what?"

"Claymore. A Scottish sword of the medieval period. William Wallace and all those fun people. Didn't you see *Braveheart*? Mel Gibson saving Scotland. It's right up your macho alley."

"Sorry. I missed that bloodletting. I didn't know you were an expert on swords."

"I'm not. But I have high-speed web service. Claymores have three to four feet long blades and hilts that can be a foot to a foot and a half, with a pommel for balance and a crosspiece guard. They are usually sharp on both edges and the point, the blade is around two inches wide or more, and they are used two-handed, usually swung like a baseball bat as a cutting blade. A strong man who knows how to use one can cut a person in half with one swing. They're not fun at parties."

"No, I guess not. But if it's actually a medieval sword, it should be easy to trace."

"You can buy replicas online for anywhere from $100 to $600. There's a market for them as movie props, theatre props, and for those 'reenactor' groups."

"Just what we need, freaks walking around with six-foot swords."

"Well, at least you can see what kills you."

"Not much consolation in my book. Anyway, do you want to talk to the guy who called this in? He's the director of this student center."

"Yeah, sure. Bring him in."

Robert signaled to the police officer controlling the back door to the building that opened into a small parking lot out back. After a moment, a man in a white dress shirt and black slacks entered and crossed to Robert. He was in his early thirties, only about five foot six, and had a withered left arm. He kept trying not to look at the naked bodies on the ping-pong table but managed to fail several times.

"This is Reverend Mike Lang, the Director of the Baptist Student Union at U of A. This is Detective Dayton."

Kate shifted position so that her back was to the dead women, forcing the minister to either look at her eyes, her chest, the floor, or the naked bodies. He managed to take in all four within a couple of seconds. He started to extend his hand for a handshake, but she pulled out her notebook and pen, filling her hands, leaving him standing there awkwardly. She pointed to his awkwardly positioned arm.

"Polio?"

"Yeah, when I was a kid. During a trip to the Middle East. My parents didn't believe in vaccines."

"Sorry."

"Me too. It took a few years, but everything recovered except the arm. It's not totally useless, but it's weak."

"You made the 911 call?"

"Yes."

"Tell me about it."

"Well, I got here a few minutes after ten. The center doesn't open on Mondays until eleven, but I wanted some time to set up a few things. I have a parking spot out back, so I came in the back door, came down the little hall, and saw, well, that. I just dropped my briefcase and walked over to make sure it was real."

"Did you touch anything?"

"No."

"Not even to see if they were dead?"

"Oh, that was easy to see."

"Then?"

"I unlocked my office, there, at the corner of the back hall, and went in and used the landline to call 911. They had me stay on the line, so I stood there in the office door until I heard the police knocking on the front door and I went to open that. After they saw, well, you know, what they saw, one of them escorted me outside to wait until everybody else showed up. I did call my wife on my cell phone, then talked to this other detective when he got here. Otherwise, I've just been outside trying to work from my car."

"Do you recognize either of the decedents?"

"The dead women? Well, I never really got a look at their faces, you know, they're, you know, sort of hidden. But, no, I don't think I know them."

"Not somebody who comes here?"

"No. At least I hope not."

"But the building was locked when you got here?"

"Yes. I used my key to get in and I heard the lock turn. And the security system was on. There's a keypad just inside the door. I have to enter a code within sixty seconds. I saw the light go from red to green."

"And the front door?"

"Well, turning off one alarm turns them both off, but I had to turn the deadbolt knob on the inside to let the police in. It was definitely locked."

"Any other ways in, windows, through the kitchen I see over there maybe?"

"No. No other doors. The windows don't open. We're totally dependent on the air conditioner. Last time it broke we had to close down for a day. Place was an oven."

"Who has keys?"

"Me, my wife has one we keep at home, just in case. The student president of the group has one, but he's not supposed to be here without me at night."

"Your wife still has her key?"

"Yes. I asked her to check when I called her. It was just where we keep it."

"And the security code? Who has that?"

"Same three people, but we don't exactly hide it when we come in with somebody. I guess there are several people who could have watched one of us enter it and figured it out. Past student presidents would have it too, but not a key. Unless they made a copy and didn't tell me."

"This current student president got a name?"

"Lloyd Ellison. He's a grad student in philosophy. I gave his number to this other detective."

"I'm not a Baptist, Reverend. Tell me about this place."

"Well, most of the major denominations have some kind of student organization at the really big universities. Outreach, service, mission; it goes by all kinds of names. Basically, we try to help Baptists, and any other student that wants to join us, while they are at college. We give them a place to hang out, hang around with other students like themselves. We have lots of social activities; Wednesday night hot dog dinners, Friday movie screenings, occasional speakers, pot-luck dinners around holidays. We have Bible studies that are more group counseling than serious theology. I also lend a sympathetic ear to kids who find the pressures of academics or growing up a bit much sometimes. Basically, trying to give them an alternative to drinking parties and sex parties; that kind of thing. We also do a lot of under-the-table helping out. Some of these kids would have to look a long way up to see the poverty line. A lot of the food churches give us never makes it to the group dinners but gets quietly passed to kids who wouldn't eat without it. We also have a little closet with some spare clothes from various sources that get discreetly given out when we see somebody without a sweater or shoes all worn out or something. And I've quietly made arrangements for a couple of students who had no place to go for long holidays when the dorms are closed, found families willing to have a guest, that kind of thing. We do a lot of good that never gets noticed."

"Doing all this good make any enemies?"

"Well, Baptists, I'm sorry to say, don't always have the best reputation on college campuses. It doesn't say it on the sign out front, but this is a 'Southern Baptist'-supported student center. It's a rather conservative denomination, even compared to some other Baptists. We have a history of coming down on the wrong side of lots of the segregation stuff, though at least we admit it now. But we don't have women ministers yet, no gay marriages in the church, not too open to gays in general. Definitely pro-life. But here, we try to stay away from the political stuff. We know the students we have here are all over the map politically. We don't want to turn anybody off to religion. Some of the churches around town and across the country are more activists in their social stances, but here we try to focus on what individual students need, spiritually, socially, or physically and avoid saying we have all the answers to the political problems. As far as I know, nobody hates us enough to want to kill us. Or whatever finding two dead naked women in here is going to do to us."

"So, you're not really a part of the university."

"No. The Baptist State Conference owns the land and pays my salary, plus provides a bare-bone budget. Some of the area churches chip in too. Part of my job is fundraising to cover some of the help for students and some of the presentations and social activities that the budget doesn't cover."

"When was the last time the building was open?"

"Saturday night. We didn't have much going on, but we kept the building open until eleven for people who just wanted to watch TV with friends or something. We keep it closed on Sundays so the local congregations don't see us as competition. We actually encourage the students to go to a local church on Sundays."

"So, who locked up Saturday night?"

"I did. And I'm sure I turned on the security system and locked both doors before I left. And the building was empty. I always check because sometimes we have a kid who has no place to go and tries to hide in the bathroom or something."

"Does Detective Delahey have your contact information?"

"Yes."

"Robert, you see any reason to detain Reverend Lang any longer?"

"No, I got what I need."

"I suspect we're going to need the use of your building most of the day, but we'll call you when you can get back in. A patrol officer will be here until you can come back to lock up."

"Thank you."

"Thank you for your cooperation."

And he took one last look at the naked bodies as he walked away from her.

"See he gets out all right. I need to talk to Kelsey."

She walked over to where the ME was taking over from the techs. She stood on the table, straddling the bodies, trying to figure out how to remove the sword without creating any new cuts that might muddy the evidence.

"Kate Dayton, if you ask me for cause of death, I'm going to slap you."

"Kelsey Smith, you underestimate me."

"Yeah. So?"

"The sword blade is about four feet long. The two bodies are almost two feet thick, piled up one on top of the other. Even holding the crosspiece, standing on the table like you are, the killer would have had to have held the crosspiece at least six feet up, probably above eye level, not to mention shoulder level. Higher if they were holding it by the hilt. Then they had to plunge it straight down, hard enough to penetrate two bodies plus three-quarter plywood, all the way down to the hilt. You agree? Even if they were dead or unconscious and stacked up this way, the sword had to do all this in one stroke, right?"

Kelsey mimed doing what Kate described.

"That's what it looks like."

Kelsey gave a tentative tug upward to the hilt with her gloved hands, but it didn't move. She tried again, squatting over the bodies to bring her legs into the effort. Still no movement. She looked around the room, spotted a large police officer, gestured him over, got down from the ping-pong table, and handed him a pair of latex gloves.

"Try to pull straight up, I don't want to cut anything that hasn't already been cut, but I've got to get that sword out in order to move the bodies."

The police officer gloved up, climbed up on the table (which caused it to groan and bend a little), carefully placed one foot on each side of the dead women, squatted like a weight lifter (while trying to be sure his butt didn't touch the butt of the top woman), grabbed the hilt with both hands, and jerked upward at the same time he rose from the squat to a standing position. The sword emitted a terrifying squeal as it scrapped against the wood but came up out of the table and the two bodies. He handed the sword to the assistant ME, jumped down from the table, and took off the gloves.

"Thank you."

"I knew all that weightlifting would pay off someday."

Kelsey took her flashlight and shone it into the hole in the top body left by the sword.

"Sliced right through the spine. Probably the one below too. Death was quick, but not instantaneous. Paralysis was instantaneous though, at least below the incision. Judging by the blood spatter, I think they were alive at the time, but they may have been repositioned a little afterward, heads put back in the sex position, for example. But they were on top of one another like this when the blow was struck."

"But could you have done this, for example, or should I be looking for some six-foot-nine football lineman with experience with large swords?"

"Might not have to be six nine, but at least your height and strong—very strong—would be my first guess. Let me do some tests with the sword, how sharp it is, weight, handling, etc. But bone isn't that easy to slice through, and then to go through the wood, all in one thrust? Not easy, I bet. I'll get you more specifics after I do some tests."

"Faster may be better. This guy may have more than one sword."

"Got it."

"Can I be bold and ask for a preliminary estimate of time of death?"

"Based on rigor, probably sometime last night. I'll narrow that down later."

"Thanks."

The photographer stepped in to take more pictures as the assistant ME rolled up a gurney with a body bag and they rolled the first body off the lower one onto the gurney.

"Send me facials I can use to ask about IDs.

"You got it."

Kate turned to one of the techs.

"Where do we stand on fingerprints?"

"We sent them in and they are being run right now. No hits yet."

Robert stepped up to Kate.

"The student president who has a key is here."

"Good. Let's talk to him outside."

Kate and Robert stepped out the front door to where a patrol officer was standing next to a young man carrying a small backpack. He was thin and maybe five foot eight at the most, almost a classic nerd with glasses with wireframes and a short haircut, wearing jeans and a plaid, short-sleeved shirt. Kate nodded at the uniformed officer, and he moved away, back to crowd control, keeping the other people on the sidewalk several feet from the building.

"Lloyd Ellison?"

"Yes."

"How much do you weigh?"

"Huh? What does that matter?"

"Just humor me."

"And who are you?"

"Detective Dayton. This is Detective Delahey. We are here to either keep you out of trouble or ruin your day. Now, how much do you weigh?"

"One twenty, give or take."

"That may be a very good answer. Do you have a key to this building?"

"Right here, on my keyring. See?"

"Anybody borrow your keyring lately?"

"No."

"Maybe without you knowing?"

"I doubt it. My car key, my apartment key, even my library carrel key are on it. I have it on me whenever I'm out of my apartment."

"When were you here last?"

"At the Baptist Student Center? Friday night. We had a speaker on depression among college students. I'm not depressed, but as the president I had to be here."

"You weren't here on Saturday or Sunday?"

"No. Saturday I was in the library all day and Sunday I went to church in the morning, watched pro football in the afternoon, and went to sleep right after supper."

Kate and Robert's phones both pinged. They took out their phones and looked at the message, swiping between the two pictures they had received. Kate held up her phone so Lloyd could see the screen, swiping between both pictures.

"You know either of these women?"

"Are they dead?"

"Very. You know them?"

"No. I don't recognize either of them."

"You hadn't seen either of them here at the student center?"

"No. Who are they?"

"That's what we'd like to know."

"What happened in there?"

"We'd sort of like to know that too."

"Damn."

"Amen."

"I guess everything is canceled for the center."

"At least for today, that would be my guess."

"I've got class in fifteen minutes, should I come back after?"

"Make sure Detective Delahey has all your contact information. We'll call you if we need to talk to you again."

Kate left Robert with Lloyd Ellison and went back inside the student center. She stood there for a few moments watching the bustle as the bodies were being carried out the back door on gurneys to the waiting ME truck. Her thoughts flashed back to her college days at a very different kind of college, much smaller and far from this warm desert. After a moment, Robert came back in.

"What now?"

"It's fraternity and sorority rush season, isn't it?"

"You're asking me? I worked my way through tech school waiting tables."

"Start calling the sorority houses. The university should have a listing. Ask them if they are missing any pledges."

"You think this was some kind of hazing stunt gone wrong?"

"Just a wild guess. Humor me."

"OK, OK. I'll get a couple of people back at HQ on it too."

"Fine."

As Robert moved away to make calls, Kate looked around. With the bodies now gone, the crime scene techs had scattered to measure blood spatter and take fingerprints on any surface that looked promising. Kate walked a circle around the room. On the corner by the back hallway was the director's office, followed by the two restrooms, then the kitchen with a large pass-through window facing the all-purpose room. The back wall had three windows, but they indeed were the kind that had no way to be opened and were just to let light in. Along the next side were folding partitions that partly hid a space with a fold-down table and chairs that could be used for meals or meetings, then the TV lounge by the front hallway. On the other side of the hall was the little conference room Kate had passed on the way in, then a large closet labeled STORAGE. Past that were a couple more doors, one labeled DONATIONS and another UTILITIES, and then the rear entrance from the parking lot. She gloved up and tested the three doors, but all were locked. Not many places to hide, but may be possible.

She walked over and stared at the ping-pong table, with the void created by the bodies in the middle of all the blood. The women looked like they were college-age. Two young lives, gone in a long instant, in the middle either of an act of love, a moment of lust, or some college prank turned tragedy. She wondered what she would say to the parents, and sooner or later she would have to talk to the parents, once they found out who these two women were. "Were," a past tense coming far too soon.

Robert came back in and crossed to her.

"Got anything?"

"Not really, but we're still calling around. We're not giving out any details, just asking if any pledges or members are missing. But one of the sorority members I talked to made a strange comment."

"Yes?"

"They said most of the sororities had cut way back on the hazing, but if it was something really out of bounds it was probably the Tri-Chi's up to something."

"Come on, Delahey, get to the good part."

"Tri-Chi isn't really a sorority; it's more like a secret club. Known for being a little outrageous."

"Tri-Chi. Chi, chi, chi, written like XXX, triple X. It's a 'ch' sound in Greek. Greek has an x sound, but that's 'xi', not written like any English letter. More like three parallel horizontal lines with the top and bottom lines longer than the middle."

"How the hell do you know all that?"

"I actually stayed awake in college. Point is, they sound more like a rating for a sex film than a group of man-hungry English majors. You think there really is such a group, or is this just some urban legend?"

"Beats me. That's just what the girl I talked to said."

"Robert, if she was a university student, she was probably a woman, not a girl. Try to pretend I've taught you some manners."

"OK, OK. Sorry. The woman reported the existence of a secret student group that indulged in committing sexually adventurous events."

"Call the Dean of Women or whatever they call it here, find out what's real and what's rumor."

"Right."

Kate took one more look around, then walked out the back door to get the lay of the land around the parking lot. There were about eight parking spaces inside a walled lot, but there was no gate to close the lot off from entry. Just a sign indicating NO PUBLIC PARKING. University buildings occupied the block across the street, and the wall separated the parking lot from the area around adjacent buildings. No real barriers to entry, but not much cover either. She looked for traffic cameras or security cameras. The intersection in front just had stop signs and she didn't see any obvious cameras.

She walked back inside and found Robert.

"I didn't see any security cameras or traffic cameras, but have a uniform canvas the area for cameras and have traffic division give us anything leading to here Sunday night."

"Right. We got two TV stations, two newspapers, even the student newspaper, the *Wildcat*, clumped over there wanting a statement."

"OK. You can be famous for fifteen minutes. Tell them we have two unidentified deceased women that we are trying to identify. Don't release any pictures yet. That's no way to find out your daughter is dead. Anyone with information please call the police or the anonymous hotline. Nothing about how they died or any details at all, got it? Everything is still under investigation."

"Got it."

Robert moved away to deal with the press just as Kate's phone rang. She looked at the name of the caller and took the call.

"Chief."

"I hear you have a wild one."

"Definitely not something you run into every day."

"I'm getting calls from the head of the state Baptist group, the university president's office, even the head of the university police department."

"The crime scene is definitely off-campus, if just barely. We don't have IDs on the victims yet, but we don't think they were members of the Baptist group. We're not even sure they were students, though they look in the right age group. But we're just getting started."

"OK, got it. Don't leave me hanging, Kate."

"You know me better than that, Chief."

"OK, back to work."

"Right."

She ended the call just as a text message came in. *Prints match Betty Kay Koonce, 820 W. Calle Sur, age 18, no NOK listed.* She saw that Robert had been copied on the text. She saw that he was still busy telling the media as little as possible, so she sent him a text. *I'm headed to Registrar's Office. Call me when done here.*

She went out of the building and got back in her police cruiser. She realized she could have called the Registrar's Office, but disembodied voices tended to be ignored. When you are in a hurry, sometimes it's faster to just show up. Pulling back onto N. Euclid, she immediately turned left onto E. University and followed that to the heart of the campus. She knew that the Second Street parking garage would be full, so she stayed on E. University until she got to Highland, took a left and another left, and parked in front of the administration building on the sidewalk. Not good politics with the campus police, but this was important.

Entering the building, she saw the Registrar was in 210, went up the stairs to the second floor, pulled out her ID, and flashed it as she entered.

"I need to see the Registrar."

"He's with someone."

"Interrupt him."

She always thought it was strange that a police uniform with stripes and shiny metal bits, along with a badge and ID case, made people do as told, but she thought that usually turned out to be a good thing. As long as the police officer was telling them the right things to do. After just a second, the door opened, a couple of students stepped out, and Kate stepped in, closing the door behind her.

"Officer?"

"Detective Dayton. We have a dead woman we think may be a student here. She was murdered. I need whatever records you have on her, especially her next of kin. Her name was Betty Kay Koonce, K-O-O-N-C-E. Lived on West Calle Sur."

"You know I need some kind of proof she's dead."

Kate held up her phone with the picture of one of the dead women, though she wasn't sure which one had been Betty.

"This the Baptist Student Center stuff?"

"Please, sir. We have two dead women and we really need to know what's going on."

"Just a moment."

He turned to his computer and started tapping the keys. Kate did not sit. She looked out the window at the campus stretching out before her. She knew this was a good school, but she was glad she hadn't gone to college here. It was just too big, too many people all trying to get into the same classes and the same dorms and the same dining halls, all at the same time. Maybe for grad school, but not as some freshman away from home for the first time.

After a long minute, the Registrar evidently found what he was looking for.

"Betty Kay Koonce was a freshman. No grades yet. Residence is given as 423 East Helen Street. No phone or email listed. For next of kin, she lists 'None.'"

"None? Do you allow that? And I was told she lived on Calle Sur."

"Let me check something. You said 820 W. Calle Sur?"

"Yes."

There were more clicks and taps.

"Eight twenty West Calle Sur is the Arizona Baptist Children's Service's address. As for the next of kin, she's an adult, if she doesn't list somebody, she doesn't have to. The East Helen address would be where she was actually residing while attending classes. Let me check something else."

Again, more clicks and taps.

"Yes, she was in the Next Step program."

"Which is?"

"When an orphan turns eighteen, they become an adult and lose state financial support. 'Aging out of the system,' it's called. We have a program for Arizona residents who age out to help them on the next step in their lives. We waive tuition and fees. Some may also have a little support from other programs, but most have to work at least part-time while going to school. But Betty was evidently an orphan who really did have no next of kin, at least none she wanted to mention."

"I see."

"That's pretty much all we have, except for social security numbers and other confidential information, which we would need more documentation to produce."

"Of course. Nothing saying who the other woman killed may have been?"

"Not in our data."

"OK. Thank you."

"I hope you find the killer."

"I'm sure we will."

Kate shook his hand and left. She wasn't sure she was relieved there would be no weeping parents to explain all this weirdness to or sad that a young woman had been forced to face the adult world basically alone. And not survived.

Back at her car, she found a University of Arizona patrol car blocking her car in and a university officer standing beside it.

"This is not exactly a parking place, even for Tucson police."

"It is if you are trying to solve a murder. Now you can either get out of my way, or I'll just drive through the plaza."

The university police officer gave her a dirty look but got back in the patrol car and backed out of the way. Kate headed back down University Boulevard, hitting the speed dial on her phone as she drove. Robert answered.

"Yeah, boss."

"I'm on my way to 423 East Helen Street. That's actually where Betty lived. Meet me there. And have somebody in the office contact the Arizona Baptist Children's Services and see what they have on Betty. And we may need a search warrant for the East Helen address if nobody is home."

"Got it. Any idea where East Helen is?"

"A block north of Speedway, running parallel. Not far. Maybe five minutes, if that."

"Wait for me. You want other backup?"

"Not yet. Wear your sword-proof vest."

"Very funny."

Kate turned right on North Park, went a few blocks to Speedway, and turned left. Speedway was a main thoroughfare, so it was only a couple of minutes, even with the traffic, before she turned right, went one block, and turned left onto Helen Street. In the middle of the block, she pulled to the curb and looked around. She saw a light brown stucco house next to the alley that split the block. It looked like something from the 1950s or before that had been repeatedly updated. It was a duplex, with two identical walkways and front entrances. One side bore the house number, 421, by the minuscule porch, while the other was labeled 426. That meant that 423 would be in the back, probably with a 425 on the other side. A glance at Google Maps confirmed her suspicion; in the back was a U-shaped extension with a tiny plaza between and parking spaces beyond. Glancing around, Kate saw that she was directly behind the Tucson First Baptist Church, a massive edifice of several large buildings that, including the parking lot, took up most of the block between Helen and Speedway. *These Baptists keep popping up,* she thought. *Wonder if that means anything.*

Just then, Robert pulled up behind her, got out of his car, went to the trunk, opened it, pulled out his bulletproof vest, and put it on. She got out of her car and crossed to him.

"Good, I'll let you break down the door and rush the killer."

"Sword may not be the only weapon he has."

"Don't assume it's a he."

"Sorry. Females can be just as cruel as males. I keep forgetting."

"Just don't leap to assumptions about anything."

"OK, OK."

"Four twenty-three is around back. It looks like we have to go down the alley. U-shaped in the back. Maybe two apartments back there. Four twenty-three is probably on the west side, but that's not for sure. And we have no idea who might be in 425."

"Right."

They walked up the sidewalk and then turned into the dirt alley used by trash trucks and people getting to parking areas behind their houses. As they came around the back of the house, they were a little surprised by a set of stairs leading down into the ground, with a fiberglass overhang providing shade and preventing the rare rain from getting in the hole the steps created. Peering down the steps they saw a door, an entrance to yet another apartment, this one mostly underground. Then there was a tiny plaza, and a couple of steps on either side leading up to other doors. The one on the right was labeled 423 and the one on the left was labeled 425, as expected. Robert went up to 423 and knocked.

"Tucson Police! Open up!"

There was no answer. Kate was watching the other apartment across the way, but saw no motion, no one peeking between the curtains. Robert knocked again.

"Anybody home? Police!"

There was still no reply. Robert tried to look through the window near the door, but the blinds were closed tight.

"Can't see anything."

"Where do we stand on the search warrant?"

"I'll check."

He pulled out his phone and called the station. As they were waiting, someone came around the corner of the house. He was in his twenties, about the same height as Kate, but thin as a rail, dressed like a student of the low-income persuasion, and carried a three-ring binder. He stopped when he saw Kate in her uniform and Robert in his vest.

"Is there a problem, Officer?"

"You live here?" asked Kate.

"Downstairs."

"What's your name?"

"Allen Wrenn."

"You know who lives in this apartment, Allen?"

"A couple of girls."

"Do you know their names?"

"No."

"They live right above you, and you don't even know their names?"

"I barely have seen them. I'm not home a lot."

"You go to the university?"

"Yes."

"Do they? The women?"

"I guess. Not sure."

"I find it a little surprising a healthy young man like you wouldn't even have tried to meet two young women who lived directly above him."

"I'm in theatre. I go to class during the day, in rehearsal or performance most nights. Most of my socializing, what there is of it, is with other theatre people."

"You're here now."

"Are they?"

"No, evidently not."

Kate took out her phone and pulled up the pictures of the dead women.

"Is one of these women somebody who lives here?"

"Are they dead? They look dead."

"Yes, they are very dead. Do you recognize either one?"

"They could be the two who live here, but I wouldn't swear to it. I've only seen them in passing a couple of times. Never spoke."

"They both live here?"

"Maybe. I think two women live above me, and it could be those two, but I can't say for sure. Listen, if you just want to know their names, I've got the landlord's phone number down in my apartment. He could tell you."

"Yes, that would help."

Allen walked down the steps to his door. Kate followed him.

"Watch out for the black widow."

Kate looked down and saw a black spider in the center of a web in the corner of one of the stone steps. She carefully stepped around it.

"They like the shade."

"They don't bother you?"

"I mind my business, they mind theirs. I take the middle, they take the corner. I don't see any need to kill something just because I don't like it. They're not that dangerous anyway."

"So I've heard."

He unlocked his door and stepped into the little apartment. Kate followed and stopped in the doorway, seeing that it would be crowded if they were both inside. He dropped his notebook on the single bed that took up the entire right wall and turned to his desk on the other side which barely held a small keyboard and monitor. A folding chair functioned as the desk chair. Beside it was a metal wardrobe, which, with the desk and a stack of boxes, took up the left wall. In between, on the far wall, was a chest of drawers, topped by the smallest television Kate had seen in years and a small printer. She looked around the door and saw the entrance to a bathroom not much bigger than a shower stall. Beside it was the entrance to a tiny kitchen, without even a door. In fact, there was no stove, only a two-burner hotplate on a minuscule table, a refrigerator that did not even look five feet tall with a loaf of bread on top, a free-standing shelf unit with big boxes of Cheerios and Rice Krispies and some cans of various beans, and a sink so small she could not have even washed her cooking pans in it.

Allen had pulled a notebook out of a desk drawer and a sheet of printer paper off his desk and written something on the paper. He took one step to Kate and handed her the paper. It held a name and phone number.

"He lives not far away if you need him here, but he owns several buildings like this, little apartment complexes, so you'll have to tell him what you want."

"Thank you."

"Do I need to clear out for a while, or can I grab some lunch and a nap before heading back for rehearsal?"

"I'm not expecting any gunfights. As long as you stay inside, it shouldn't be a problem."

"Thanks."

"Thank you. And what's the saying, 'break a leg'?"

"That's it. Thanks."

Kate stepped out, closing the door behind her. She heard him lock the deadbolt from inside. She checked that the spider was still on its web and climbed the stairs up to ground level, wondering what life was like for Allen Wrenn.

Back up on the plaza, Robert was still on the phone.

"Nothing yet. Can't find a judge not in session this time of day."

"Our friend downstairs says two women live here that might be the two victims. I guess we really need to find out who the other one is. I'll try the landlord."

Kate took out her phone and entered the number on the piece of paper.

"I'm trying to contact Regan Maroney, the landlord for 423 E. Helen."

"This is Regan Maroney."

"Mr. Maroney, I'm Detective Kate Dayton from the Tucson Police Department. We need access to one of your apartments, specifically 423 E. Helen. We believe the renter may be deceased."

"What? She's dead? In the apartment?"

"No, we believe she died elsewhere. We're trying to confirm identity."

"I'll be there in fifteen minutes."

"Thank you."

The call was terminated.

"Landlord will be here in fifteen minutes."

"OK."

"If he confirms one of the residents is Betty Koonce, he has the authority to let us in."

"OK. So we just cool our heels?"

"Call the office and see if anybody has come up with anything. And did you ever get anything from the Dean of Women?"

"She says she thinks Tri-Chi is a myth, or at least not something really organized. If something really sexy and scandalous happens around campus, the rumor is that Tri-Chi was behind it. Not a real thing, but something enough people have heard of that freshmen might be convinced it was real. Especially if somebody was trying to talk them into doing something daring. But if enough people believe it, doesn't that almost make it real?"

"You'll have to take that up with the philosophy major."

"OK. I'll check with the office."

He moved into the shade and made his phone call. Kate heard her stomach growl and realized it was getting into the afternoon. She tried to remember if she had a protein bar or something in her car but wasn't sure enough to leave Robert alone to go look. She moved into the shade beside him. It wasn't that hot this late in the year, but shade was better than sunshine in

Tucson. She thought about the theatre major downstairs and the two women upstairs who had evidently never even spoken and what that meant. She didn't consider it a good sign. After a couple of minutes, Robert hung up his phone.

"Kelsey says 'Don't be ridiculous.' The lab guys say they'll let you know as soon as they have something. The Baptists Children's Services is trying to find somebody authorized to speak to the police. And the tip line says it's Aimee Semple McPherson and Amelia Earhart."

"Nah, they were too young to be Aimee or Amelia."

"Any chance we get lunch today?"

"Not looking that way, but we'll see how this pans out."

Robert went back to his phone, and Kate began to consider the possibility that the two women could have been manipulated into believing that the Tri-Chi's were real and they were participating in some qualifying event. But that still seemed farfetched. A few minutes crawled past and a car came up the alley and pulled into the parking area behind the house. A short, bald, overweight man well past retirement age got out of the car carrying a tablet computer and crossed to them. Kate checked her watch; twelve minutes, good time. As he approached, she noticed he was eyeing her chest.

"Are you Regan Maroney?"

"Yes."

"Could I see some ID, please?"

Regan tucked his tablet under one arm and pulled out his wallet, handing Kate his driver's license.

"You said you were a detective, but that looks like Assistant Commander insignia to me. I walked a beat for a couple of years, way back in the day."

Kate examined the license and saw that it matched the man in front of her. She passed it to Robert, who recorded some of the information and handed it back to Regan.

"'Detective' is enough for most circumstances. You own this building?"

"Yes, this and three others. Twenty rental units in all. I'm not getting rich, but with the social security and a little retirement, I'm getting by."

Kate took out her phone and showed him the two pictures.

"You recognize either of these women?"

"Are they dead? They are dead, aren't they?"

"Yes. Do you know them?"

"It's Betty Koonce and Donna Smith. They shared this apartment."

"Do you have next of kin information for them?"

"I don't think so, but let me check."

He turned on his tablet and navigated to rental agreement forms for his apartments.

"Not for Betty. She said she was an orphan. They only took the apartment in August. As for Donna, let's see. No, not for her either."

"What about a previous address for either of them?"

"Uh, for Betty it's 820 West Calle Sur here in Tucson. For Donna, let's see, 4001 E. Paisano Drive, El Paso, Texas 79905."

"What else can you tell me about them?"

"Well, they said they were both students at the university, freshmen just starting out. Not to be sexist, but they were both nice to look at, if you know what I mean."

"Any idea where they got the money to pay your rent?"

"They said they were both on scholarships of some kind. I think Donna did some modeling up at the university."

"Modeling?"

"For the art classes. Life drawing, photography classes, that kind of thing. Maybe some for students working on art projects, that kind of thing."

"Nude modeling?"

"Not all her modeling, but some. At least that was the impression I got."

"She ever do any erotica or that kind of thing?"

"Not that I know of, but it wasn't my business, you know."

"What about Betty, any modeling or other sources of income?"

"Not that I know of. I mean, I rented them the apartment in August, had to make a few changes because there were two of them. This apartment is usually a single. Also had to make a couple of plumbing repairs in September. I only talked to them a few times. I don't hang around hitting on my renters."

"Who else lives in this building?"

"Uh, let me look. Let's see, Allen Wrenn has the basement apartment. He's a grad student in theatre. He's been here over a year now. Quiet kid. Other side is Lenelle Davison, music major from Phoenix. She's new too. She's a junior but was in the dorms her first two years. She has an electric keyboard but uses head-phones so she doesn't bother anybody. The front two apartments are bigger, built for two people. A couple of guys, Sean Heumann and Richard Walker have 421. English majors, seniors this year. I think they're gay, but that's not my concern. Four twenty-six is two women, Pamela Sandacz and Barbara Maddox. Sophomores here to party and definitely not lesbians, but they keep it quiet in the apartment. That's about all I know, except they all pay their rent on time."

"Can you let us in?"

"Can I see your IDs and get your cards?"

Kate and Robert pulled out their police ID folders and hand-ed Regan a business card with their contact information at the office. Regan stuffed the cards in his shirt pocket and pulled out a key ring to open the door.

"Give the key to Detective Delahey."

Regan found the right key, took it off the key ring, and hand-ed it to Robert. Robert went to the door and unlocked it but did not enter.

"This is going to take a while. The lab techs will have to do their thing inside. We'll call you when you can come back and pick up the key."

Regan did not look happy with being dismissed, but he took the hint and went back to his car and drove away. Robert opened the door to the apartment but stood back to let Kate enter first. Being very careful not to touch anything, she took a couple of steps inside and looked around. Robert stood in the doorway to call the lab techs to come run the apartment.

Kate saw that the room was a combination kitchen, dining, and living area. It wasn't very big, but at least it had a small stove with an actual oven. There was a table that could sit four, but there were only two chairs. There was a small sofa that looked like a Goodwill reject. There were blinds in the windows, but no curtains. There was no TV, no decorations on the walls, no family pictures of any kind. Putting on latex gloves, Kate opened the cabinets and saw a few cans of food and some bags of dried beans and a bag of rice, along with boxes of cereal and noodles. The refrigerator did have a gallon of milk and some leftovers, but little else. To the right were a hallway and a small bathroom. There was a shower, but no tub. The medicine chest had a little makeup and some Midol. Down the hall was the bedroom, without even a door to separate it from the kitchen area. There were two single beds, two chests of drawers, and a small closet. There were clothes hanging in the closet, but it seemed like not very many for two women. On the floor were two large duffel bags that evidently had contained all the clothes and personal items of the two women. There was one small laptop on one bed and another laptop on top of one of the dressers. Those might have lots of information in their emails, but the passwords would have to be cracked first, so Kate left them where they were. She didn't see any cell phones; evidently, those were wherever the women's clothes and purses were. Wherever that was. Robert came up behind her.

"Not much of anything, is there?"

"I guess orphans travel light."

"You think they were both orphans?"

"I wouldn't be surprised."

"So you won't be surprised when I tell you I looked up Donna Smith's address on Google Maps."

"Vacant lot?"

"El Paso Zoo."

"Well, at least that shows a sense of humor."

"Do you think she was even from El Paso?"

"Heaven knows. But at least that might explain why we didn't get a hit on the fingerprints right away."

"Not much to learn here until the computer geeks get into the laptops."

"Actually, there's a lot to learn here from there being so little here. Two women, at least one an orphan, crammed into an apartment built for one. Bare minimum of clothing, almost no decoration, very little personal stuff. What does that tell you?"

"They were poor."

"In more ways than one. Life does not seem to have been kind to our young women. I'm amazed they were even trying to go to college instead of giving up and just waiting tables or whatever."

"The modeling may have been an easy way out. They may have been doing more than life drawing classes."

"Maybe."

"You think they were modeling for somebody on top of the ping-pong table?"

"They had separate beds, so evidently they weren't sleeping together here."

"That would explain who the third person in the room was and why they were holding still with somebody standing over them on the table while they were going at it. He probably had the sword in a tripod case or something."

"Possible. Don't close your mind to other possibilities yet. Come on; let's wait for the lab techs outside. This place makes me sad."

"Yeah."

They went back onto the plaza. As they exited, Kate's phone rang. She looked at the number and responded.

"Yeah, Tom?"

"I got a woman who says she was Betty Koonce's case manager on the line."

"Tell her we need her to identify the body. She should go to the ME's office as soon as possible. And tell her to bring Betty's case file."

"Right."

Kate disconnected.

"Office is sending Betty's case manager to the morgue to identify the body."

"So go. I can wait for the lab techs."

"Text me when you're clear. And call Kelsey and tell her who's on the way, then have somebody in the office contact El Paso and see if they have anything on Donna Smith who claimed to live in the zoo."

"Right."

The medical examiner's office was basically due south of the university, near the Banner University Hospital Medical Center complex, but it was actually faster to continue west on Speedway and hop on I-10 East to the Palo Verde exit and then circle back a few blocks to East District Street. Kate was there well before the case manager, who had to come from Calle Sur on the north side of Tucson. Kate went straight to the morgue, where she found Kelsey preparing the bodies for an identification viewing, covering the bodies with sheets so only the heads could be uncovered if desired. There was also the claymore and some now-sheered animal bone and wood.

"Looks like you've been busy."

"That claymore is a hell of a weapon."

"Tell me something I don't know."

"It's a replica. Manufacturer's name is engraved on the blade just under the crosspiece, but I haven't found a serial number yet. But it's high-grade steel, and it's been honed to almost razor sharp, and I mean that literally. Under a microscope, you can see the marks showing it's sharper now than it was when it left the factory."

"Interesting. And?"

"And you were right about the position. The angle of the thrust shows it was made from almost directly above, one downward stab. And you were right that means that whoever did it was standing astride the two bodies. And while somebody your size might be able to get it through one or even one and a half bodies and spines, it would be a lot easier if the killer was taller, so they could get some momentum with the sword before hitting the first body. And being strong would really help. But as sharp as it is, you don't need to be Mr. Universe."

"But definitely a mister?"

"I'd put my money on a tall male that lifts weights or does heavy physical labor."

"And they were alive and conscious at the time?"

"I sent blood and tissue samples to the lab to be sure, but I would be surprised if they were drugged or anything. I think they just didn't see it coming because of where their faces were—if you get the idea."

"They knew somebody was standing over them, but didn't think they were about to get that kind of penetration."

"You put it so politely."

"Any evidence of the other kind of penetration?"

"No, but I took swabs anyway."

"Of course. Did they have time to do anything after?"

"The one on top, just looking at where the sword went in, probably died pretty quickly. I'll have to get in there to be more precise. It not only would have severed the spine, but damaged the lungs and liver, not to mention cutting all kinds of veins and arteries. The one on the bottom got it more in the guts as well as the spine, just as deadly, but a little slower to bleed out. And stuck to the table by the sword and with their lower bodies paralyzed, they couldn't move much. Not to mention the one on the bottom had a dying body on top of her. And any movement would have just made things worse, since the sword was still in them. The heads, arms, and upper bodies were repositioned a little, probably after death, but basically just to put them back where they had been the instant before."

"Yuck."

"To use the medical term, ultra-yuck."

There was a knock on the door signaling that a person was there to identify the body.

"Let me talk to her first, then I'll bring her in."

"Ready here."

Kate went out into the little waiting room just outside the viewing area. There was a young woman, late twenties or early thirties, blond from a bottle but not outrageous. Clothes were conservative business attire. Kate noticed a large diamond ring on the left hand that was holding a file folder up in front of her chest as if for protection.

"I'm Detective Dayton. And you are?"

"Oh, uh, Liza James, Arizona Baptist Children's Services."

Liza went rooting in her purse and came up with a business card, which she handed to Kate. Kate glanced at it.

"You're a social worker?"

"Yes."

"And Betty Koonce's case manager?"

"For her last two years, yes."

"Mrs. James, we have two bodies in there. We think one is Betty."

"And she's dead?"

"Yes. Definitely dead. If you know of a next of kin or anyone else who would be better at identifying the body . . ."

"No. There's not really anyone else."

"Come this way, please."

Kate opened the door and let Liza into the viewing area. Kelsey uncovered the face of one body.

"No, that's not Betty."

Kelsey covered the face back up and stepped to the next table. She uncovered that face.

"Yes, that's Betty Koonce."

"You're sure?"

"Yes. That's her."

Kelsey covered the face back up and Kate led Liza back to the waiting room.

"Please, sit down."

Liza sat in one of the chairs and Kate pulled a chair over to face her.

"Would you like a Kleenex?"

"No, thank you. That won't be necessary."

"When was the last time you saw Betty?"

"In August. On her birthday. The day she aged out, she was gone. Her decision. Not that we could have stopped her. She became an adult in the eyes of the law—and had the right. I had helped her get the tuition waiver at the university, and she said she would get a job and go to school. But she never returned any calls or emails once she was gone."

"Tell me about her."

"Betty was . . . damaged. She had a family until she was thirteen. Then her father evidently was driving a little too fast out on I-10. Single car crash. No real reason was ever determined. Killed both her parents and her older sister. Betty spent months in and out of the hospital; had to have several surgeries. Her father had been a Baptist minister, so we took her in."

"No relatives?"

"Her mother was an only child, her parents dead. Her father's father had died of a heart attack, and his mother had early-onset Alzheimer's. There was a brother of Betty's father, her uncle, but he was having to take care of his mother and said he couldn't take Betty too. Looking back, that doesn't make sense to me since Betty could have helped take care of her grandmother, but that was the decision at the time. The brother developed cancer and died about a year ago, just a couple of weeks before his mother succumbed to the Alzheimer's. More distant relatives also said they just couldn't. We had hoped somebody from her father's congregation would take her in, but for some reason, nobody stepped forward."

"So, she's been in an orphanage ever since?"

"Oh, no. All the previous case managers tried to get her into a foster situation. She was too old for much chance of adoption, but we thought we could find a foster family."

"But?"

"It just never worked out. We'd find a family, but after a few weeks or months, it just wouldn't work and she would have to come back. It was never the same reason, changing financial circumstances, personality conflicts, just dealing with a teenager, all kinds of reasons. But, off the record, I think sometimes that was just an excuse. I wasn't there of course, but reading between the lines of the previous case manager reports."

"How many case managers are we talking about?"

"Four, counting me."

"In five years?"

"It's a burn-out job. Too many sad people, hopeless cases. You either move up or move out."

"I have been told that Betty was 'nice to look at.'"

"Oh, yes, she was pretty, beautiful even. But I think that may have been part of the problem in the foster homes, worried wives, that kind of thing. But that wasn't the only thing. I mean, Betty was just angry. We got her counseling, of course, but the counselors said she would never talk about what was going on before the accident. Claimed she didn't remember. But they weren't sure they believed that. Then her relatives not stepping in, nobody from the congregation taking her in, all the failed foster placements. I'm sure it was soul-killing. She had a lot to be angry about. It didn't make dealing with her easy sometimes."

"Do you know anything about her sexuality?"

"You mean was she sexually active? Not in our care. We have separate dorms for boys and girls, everybody has a roommate, and there are live-in dorm parents twenty-four seven. And I really doubt anything happened during any of the foster placements, no matter what any of the wives thought; her last one was almost two years ago, so she would have been a minor during most of them. Now since she left, well, who knows? Kids go off to college and try things out. We tried to raise her right; we're a Christian organization. We do care about them. But she was an adult and chose her own path."

"I was thinking more about her sexual orientation."

"You mean like lesbian? Not as far as I know. There's nothing in the case notes from either the case managers or the counselors about that."

"Would you know?"

"Well, probably not. You know the Bible . . . well, we think that kind of thing is a sin, and that's no big secret. Betty would have known she would not have received a favorable response if she had shown any signs along those lines. So, no, if she was, we probably wouldn't have known. Was she?"

"We don't know. The circumstances are not clear yet."

"What circumstances?"

"That's still under investigation. Is there anything else you can tell me about Betty that would help me?"

"Oh, not that I can think of. She was beautiful to look at but was one of those people God seems to have something against. What happened once she got out of our care, I have no idea."

"Did she have any friends back at the orphanage I could talk to?"

"Well, her roommates didn't seem to make it very long either. Mostly it was they got foster placements or even adopted, but some asked to move in with other people when a bed became open. There's a lot of turnover, which is good because it means we're getting kids into homes, but it doesn't make for long-term friendships among the kids."

"I see. The other woman in there, you didn't recognize her?"

"No. As far as I know, I've never seen her before."

"Does the name Donna Smith mean anything to you?"

"Donna Smith, Donna Smith. That's so generic, but somehow it rings a bell. Oh, yes, back in July I got an email from a colleague in Texas. She had a case that was aging out and had been admitted to the University of Arizona. She was asking if I had any contacts who could help her get a reasonable apartment near the campus or maybe advise her on how to survive Tucson. Oh, bad choice of words. Sorry. Anyway, I think the case may have been named Donna Smith."

"Did you put her in contact with Betty?"

"I may have included Betty as one of several people I forwarded an edited version of the email to. I don't know if Betty contacted Donna or not."

"And you never met Donna?"

"Never met her; never even talked to her or had any direct contact."

"OK. I need a copy of Betty's case file. Since she's dead, most of the privacy laws no longer apply. If you have a problem with that, contact your supervisor and we can get a warrant. You can use the copy machine here. There will also be some paperwork the ME needs you to sign. If you wait here, someone will bring that to you in a moment. And thank you for your time."

"I'm just sorry it was her."

"So am I."

Kate went to the door and signaled Kelsey, who came out with the required documents.

"She needs access to the copy machine."

"Fine."

Kate went back to her car and checked her phone. There was a text from Robert saying he had left the apartment to the techies. She called him.

"Anything new?"

"Nothing obvious to the tech team. El Paso says they have a Donna Smith in the driver's license database living at a children's home in El Paso, not the zoo. Anything on your end?"

"I'm beginning to ask God to save me from Baptists. But we have a confirmed ID as Betty Koonce. Is El Paso going to send something we can confirm ID with?"

"They gave us the contact info on the children's home, and Joe is calling them, probably about right now."

"Kelsey says to put our money on a tall man with big muscles, as expected. Any idea where that student center director is about now?"

"Not really. You want me to find out?"

"Why else would I ask?"

"Sorry. I'm on it."

Kate ended the call and started driving back to the Baptist Student Center, going on the city streets instead of the interstate this time, partly because she wanted to see the variety of neighborhoods and partly because it gave her a little more time to think about how different lives can turn out, often based on things that are totally out of our control. It was not a cheery thought, and she had to practice some deep breaths as she drove to get her mind back on the case instead of the people caught up in it. As she was driving, Robert called.

"He's back at the student center. The scene was just released, and he called in a cleaning crew."

"Meet me there."

"On my way."

She continued back to the location just off campus and parked until Robert's car pulled up nearby. She got out and met him on the way to the door. The door was locked, but she could hear the cleaning crew and various equipment sounds inside; she knocked loudly.

"Mr. Lang! Tucson police!"

After a moment, Mike Lang came to the door and unlocked it.

"We need to talk."

"It's a little noisy in here."

"Step out here."

Mike stepped outside, letting the door close behind him, blocking most of the noise except for the cars going by.

"Is there a problem?"

"I need to know if you have any unusually tall people at your center."

"Unusually tall? What's this about?"

"Just answer the question, please."

"I don't want to get anybody into trouble."

"You had two dead women in your center this morning; there's already trouble."

"OK, OK. There're several men about six foot one, six foot two, but the only really tall one is Garnett Bartels."

"How tall is he?"

"I'm not sure, six foot seven, six foot eight. Big guy. He's on the football team. Offensive line. We don't see him much in the Fall because of all the games and practices and stuff, but he comes around a lot in the Spring."

"How could we find him?"

"Well, he lives in one of the athletes' dorms on campus. I've got his email, I guess."

"What about a room number or a phone number?"

"I don't think so. Like I said, he's not exactly a regular."

"But he's been here several times?"

"Sure. Lloyd Ellison might have his number; they have this odd Felix and Oscar-type relationship. They hang out sometimes, though why they get along is a mystery to me. They have this stunt where Garnett picks Lloyd up by his neck with one hand. Freaks me out."

"But he's on the university football team?"

"Right."

"Thank you, Mr. Lang. You can go back to cleaning up your mess now."

"Right."

Kate and Robert walked back to her car.

"Now, if I were a football player, where would I be this time of day?"

"If you were a football player? Frankly, boss, I don't think the shoulder pads would fit."

"Very funny. Let me rephrase that. Where would a University of Arizona football player be this time of day?"

"Probably at practice, or at least some kind of team meeting, film study, something like that."

"But probably not in his room."

"Probably not."

"Let's find the coach first, try to find out more about Garnett Bartels."

"The football offices are at the end of the stadium. I think there's a staff parking lot right by it. Otherwise, you have to park several blocks away."

"I think they can make us honorary staff for an hour or two. You lead; I'll be right behind you."

This time they went down Euclid to Sixth and turned east. Left on Highland and then right on Fourth, then a right into the little parking lot. At the north end of the Arizona Stadium was the Lowell-Stevens Football Facility. Following a few signs and asking a couple of questions of passersby got them to the Head Coach's office. A secretary guarded the entrance to anything past the anteroom. Kate flashed her badge and ID again.

"I need to see the coach."

"Which one?"

"The main one."

"He's busy right now."

"Interrupt him."

"Can I say what this is about?"

"One of his players."

The secretary picked up the phone and pressed a button.

"The police are here about one of the players."

There was a pause.

"Yes, sir. He wants to know which one."

"That's confidential."

"She won't say. Yes, sir. He says there are more than one hundred players on the team and he has a meeting in five minutes. Can you at least tell him offense or defense?"

"Offensive line. And if I don't see somebody in two minutes he will be under arrest for impeding a murder investigation."

"Offensive lineman, it's about a murder, and she's getting angry. Yes, sir. He says thirty seconds."

It was more like a minute, but then a young man who looked like a football player past his playing days came running down the hall into the anteroom.

"You're not the head coach."

"I'm the Assistant Offensive Line coach. If this is about an offensive lineman, I'm the one you need to talk to."

"What's your name?"

"Gordon Gray."

"Is there someplace we can talk privately?"

"This way."

He led Kate and Robert down the hallway to a small office that barely had a desk and a couple of chairs.

"Let me get another chair."

"Don't bother. This won't take long."

"This is about a murder?"

"Tell me about Garnett Bartels."

"Uh, six foot seven, two-seventy. Fifth-year senior. Was a second-string guard, but he messed up his knee during Spring practice last semester, so when he tried to make a comeback, we moved him to tackle. He's still not as mobile as he needs to be; right now he's third on the depth chart for right tackle."

"So not one of your stars headed to the pros."

"No. He never even was a starter, even before the injury. His football career is basically over."

"What's he like as a person?"

"Well, you know, competitive on the field, not so much off it. OK guy, not the sharpest tool in the shed."

"How so?"

"He spends a lot of time at the academic center getting some extra help with classes. The tutors there know him well."

"Where is he now?"

"Right now? No idea. But he's due for a meeting of the offensive linemen in thirty minutes."

"Where will that be?"

"Downstairs in one of the film rooms."

"I'm not sure that's a good idea."

"We have to have our meetings."

"Coach Gray, causing me problems is the definition of a bad idea. Obstructing justice is a crime, and I mean that literally."

"What if I bring him here as soon as he comes in? Would that work for you? Causing a ruckus in a room full of three-hundred-pound men full of testosterone after they lost two days ago is not a good idea."

"OK, fine. In the meantime, I need to know where he lives and to talk to one of those tutors who knows him so well."

"Sure, sure."

The coach picked up the phone and pushed a button.

"I need the personal file on Garnett Bartels, and see if Andelys Ackley is around or one of the other academic advisors and send them to my office. Right. Thanks."

He hung up the phone.

"I'll be back as soon as I can find him. Did he really kill somebody?"

"Right now, we just want to talk, but we really need to talk to him right now."

"Got it."

He went out of the office and jogged down the hall. Robert watched him go.

"Not the most cooperative group."

"I guess the world will end if they lose again next Saturday."

"I guess so."

Robert looked down the hallway, which was now deserted.

"I guess everybody has gone to one meeting or another."

"Let's wait in the hall. I don't like the idea of being trapped in this little office with an offensive lineman. That could get crowded fast."

They went out into the hallway. After a couple of minutes, a woman walked toward them. She was in her thirties, brown hair to her waist, black slacks and a white shirt.

"You wanted to talk to somebody about Garnett Bartels?"

"You are?"

"Andelys Ackley. I'm in the Clements Academic Center. We help the athletes with their classes."

"Including Garnett Bartels?"

"Including Garnett."

"Tell me about him."

"He's one of our regulars. He's usually a nice guy, but not exactly academically successful. Some courses we can get him through, but others, well, not so much."

"For example?"

"Well, he wanted to get an art minor. He really likes photography, that kind of thing. But it requires a couple of courses in art history, and he just hasn't been able to pass the exams. We drilled him on flashcards of the famous artworks, but he never got higher than a sixty-five, which isn't passing."

"What's his major?"

"General Studies: Sports and Society. It's a jocks' major for players who want to go into coaching or sports communication—sports-related stuff. Or at least make academic progress toward graduation to stay eligible to play."

"How's he doing on that?"

"Well, frankly, I don't think he's going to graduate."

"Five years and he won't graduate?"

"Oh, he'll have enough hours, but even for general studies, there are a few required courses. He's tried the basic math class three times and the basic English twice. Even in the major, there's a required sports psychology class he failed the first time. We don't have crib courses, not the kind with one open-book multiple choice exam or an essay some grad assistant writes for them. The NCAA actually checks on that kind of thing. We're not the physics department, but our students have to pass college-level courses legitimately."

"And he's not going to do it?"

"I don't think so."

"What will happen to him?"

"Well, his athletic scholarship will run through the next semester. After that, who knows? Without a degree, he can't even coach in high school because you have to have teacher certification. I really don't know. He's big and strong, maybe he can work for a moving company or something."

"Do you think he knows he's not going to graduate?"

"Yeah, I think even he's figured that out. I don't really expect him to stay much after the end of football season unless it's just to have a place to stay and food to eat for a few more months. After that, who knows?"

At that moment, Coach Gray came jogging up the hall.

"One of the other players said they stopped by Garnett's room to see if he wanted to walk to the meeting, and he wasn't there, but there was a bad smell, like blood and stuff."

"Take us there right now. Robert, call for backup."

They went running down the hall, out of the building, and across the parking lot to another building, through the doors, up the stairs, and to a dorm room door that was locked. Kate stood close to the door and sniffed the air.

"What do you smell?"

"Death."

"Kick it in."

Robert stepped back and kicked the door right at the lock several times until it finally broke. Inside lay Garnett Bartels, face down, with a short, wide sword sticking through his body. A footlocker at the foot of the bed was propped open and several different types of swords were visible. Coach Gray stuck his head in and started to gag before running off to be sick elsewhere.

"Another victim?"

"We'll have to have Kelsey confirm it, but I think he fell on his sword like a noble Roman warrior. At least I think that's a Roman short sword, from what I can see of it. Collecting swords seemed to be a thing to him."

"Warrior mentality carried over from football, maybe? The crippled soldier unable to face civilian life."

"You've got to stop trying to be a psychologist.

"Yeah. I probably don't know what I'm talking about."

Kate saw a professional-type camera on the desk next to a computer, put on her gloves, picked it up, and turned it on. She began to review the photos that had already been taken.

"Betty and Donna, before and after. You can't see their faces, but it's them. I bet these pictures have already been loaded to the Web, somewhere. One last art project to leave a little mark on the world. He couldn't graduate, but he could leave something to remember him by."

"Any chance it's a setup?"

"Maybe, but I don't think so. I just think the world killed these people long before they actually died."

"How do you think he got them to pose?"

"My guess would be money, but he may have spun them some Tri-Chi hooey or something about an art assignment or something. Heaven knows."

"What a mess."

"You call Kelsey and the rest of the tech crew; I need to call the Chief. And when the backup arrives, have them block this hall off."

"Right."

"And if that football coach comes back, tell him football is not the most urgent thing in his life right now."

Dark and Bloody Ground

Daniel Boone walked this land. And he kept on walking. The Cumberland Gap, the passage through the Appalachian Mountains that Boone guided the first groups of settlers through to reach the "dark and bloody ground" of Kentucky, was a few miles east, but the settlement of Boonesboro was farther west and north. Where there was enough flatland to actually farm. Here in these mountains, flatland was rare and only found in small patches.

Instead, most settlements in this area were in the narrow valleys between ridges of worn-out mountains. Barbourville was one of those settlements, now a little town with small creeks running through. At least they were small creeks most of the time. Occasionally, they became raging torrents when rain in the mountains ran downhill all at once. Barbourville had partly solved that problem by building a levee along one side of Richland Creek, where it flowed into the Cumberland River. That kept most of the flooding on the other side, away from the town. The town was bordered on the other side by the Cumberland Gap Parkway, the modern highway that followed Boone's old path part of the way through the mountains.

In between river and road was a little town in what was known as coal country, the section of Eastern Kentucky that had made a lot of people who didn't live there rich and most of the people who did live there poor while digging out the black ore and destroying the land itself. This was a beautiful land, until the leaves fell from the trees in late fall, revealing the scars and poverty usually hidden. It made people pray for snow to soften the hard edges until new leaves could grow in the spring and hide the sadness.

Barbourville was a little different from the other little towns in the area because of Union College. Union was a small Methodist school, started back in the 1800s to help the poor whites in the mountains earn an education and perhaps a way out. It put an economic floor under the town that many other coal towns did not have as the mines went through their cycles of rise and fall. It also made Barbourville a little less extreme than the sunset towns around them. In the sunset towns, Blacks were welcome to come in during the day and spend their money, as long as they were gone by sunset. In Barbourville, there were a few places Blacks could actually reside. Heck, the town prostitute was Black.

Alan Brown knew all this because his older sister had told him. She had studied the history of the town when she moved here with her husband to teach classes at the college for a few years after they retired from Vassar. She taught physics and her husband taught math. Alan had not figured out if they were paying a penitence of some kind or really wanted to do something noble before fading into the sunset. But now her husband was dead of cancer and Alan was fulfilling his family obligations by visiting long enough to help her settle her husband's legal affairs and move to Florida. He was not a fan of this section of the country, no matter how beautiful it could be now in the summer. But while he could retire from his job, he couldn't retire from his family.

So he was just getting up from lunch with his sister in the dining room of his sister's house across the street from the college when the unmarked police car pulled up in front of the house and a plainclothes policeman got out and knocked on their door. His sister went to answer it, opening the door unasked.

"Yes?"

"Dr. Strouss, I'm Detective Sloop. I was wondering if I could have a word with your brother."

Alan got to his feet and grabbed the cane that was standing next to his chair. It was one with a tripod base that would stand on its own, as well as fold up to fit in his coat pocket when needed. There was still part of a bullet in his left knee, so he needed a little help to get around. He hobbled over to the front door to see a gaunt man with deep-set eyes and a slightly bent frame, as if malnutrition had run in his family for generations. He was wearing jeans and a black shirt, but with a badge clipped to his belt. There was a large gun in a holster on his hip.

"Yes, Officer?"

"Mr. Brown, I was told you are a big-time detective from Massachusetts."

"I don't know how 'big-time' I was, but I was a detective in Plymouth. My sister may have made me sound a little more important than I actually was. But I'm on disability retirement now. I don't get around too well anymore."

"Well, the thing is, Mr. Brown, we've got a problem right now. Frankly, it's got us buffaloed. We don't get much real crime up here, and when we do, it's fights and drunks and feuds and stuff. Not too hard to figure out who the bad guy is. But this one . . . I don't know, Mr. Brown. We're stumped and sure could use some help."

"Isn't this what the Kentucky Bureau of Investigation, or whatever name they go by, is for? To help you out?"

"It's called the Kentucky Department of Criminal Investigations. And, well, frankly, Mr. Brown, they tried. I'll give 'um that—they tried. All kinds of crime lab stuff, special agents all over the place. Nothin'. After a couple of weeks, they just packed up and went home."

"I see. And you think I could do something they couldn't?"

"When I heard about you, I looked you up online. You've got a little reputation. You come at things a different way. That seems to have worked more than once back where you come from. We're getting' pretty desperate around here. The victim was very respected at the college. We got alumni from the past thirty years breathing down our necks on this one. Anybody finds out you were here, and we didn't even ask you for help, then we'll have hell to pay."

"I see."

"I guess we can't pay as much as you would get up North, but we'll squeeze something out of the budget somewhere. You wouldn't have to solve it, just tell us where to look that we haven't already looked. Anything."

"Money is not the problem, Detective. I don't know how good a detective I was, but I was a good investor. Between the disability insurance, the settlement with the estate of the man who shot me, and what's in the investment account, I'm not hurting for money."

"Well, I'm glad to hear that, Mr. Brown. But I'm hurting for help. Just an afternoon; go over the case with me. Drive around a little to the crime scene. Like I said, tell me what to do next."

Alan turned to his sister.

"Marge?"

"Go ahead. Candice was a nice lady. Everybody at the college thought well of her. She didn't deserve what happened."

"Very well. Just let me get my hat for my bald head, Officer."

Alan took his cane and limped back to the guest room. He got his brown driver hat and a notebook small enough to fit in the pocket of his white dress shirt. Then he hobbled back to the front door. He had to use his cane to get down the three front steps and into the unmarked car. Once inside, he folded the cane into sections and laid it across his lap before putting on his seat belt.

"You set, Mr. Brown?"

"I'm ready. And if we are going to be driving around all afternoon, you can call me Alan."

"Alan. I'm Henry Sloop."

"Henry, tell me about this case, and, please, just the facts for right now."

"Sure. No problem. Well, almost three weeks ago we got a call from one of the faculty who lives over on campus saying that Candice Timm, another one of the faculty, had been found murdered in her apartment in faculty housing. That's where we're headed now. Two of our uniformed officers got there first, but I was called in as soon as they saw what was going on."

"Which was?"

"She was dead on her living room floor. Thirty-two stab wounds, two in the heart. Bloodiest thing I ever saw. Had been dead about twenty-four hours, give or take. No knife that fit the wounds anywhere around. We looked all over the apartment and the grounds around the building, but never found a thing. We found fingerprints galore all over the place, but they were all other faculty or family of faculty who had been to visit her dozens, hundreds of times."

"Anything missing?"

"Not as far as we could tell. Laptop still on the desk, phone and wallet in her purse. Cash, credit cards, ATM cards, and IDs in her wallet. A little more cash in her desk. If it was a robbery, either they ran after killing her without taking anything or they took something nobody knew she had."

"Any evidence of rape?"

"Rape? Good God, no. She must have been close to seventy years old. Had been teaching English at the college for more than forty years. Everybody loved Miss Candice. She was fully dressed when we found her, and the coroner did check, but no, no semen, no evidence of any kind of sex. She was just a nice old spinster that spent her life teaching us hill folk."

"Including you?"

"Me, no. I went to Berea College a few valleys over. 'Bout the only reason I'm the detective on the force is I've got a college degree. Lot of our officers are smart enough, but barely got out of high school. I hate to say it, but it makes a difference in keeping up with things, you know. All the technology and stuff, new ideas from outside."

"I'm sure it does."

"OK, we're turning on College Park Drive. All these houses are owned by the college."

Alan looked out at a series of modest houses, mostly from the fifties or sixties, but well maintained and occasionally updated a little. After the first few houses, the road looped into a circle with a small apartment building at the farthest part of the loop, just before it circled back to rejoin the road they were coming in on.

"And all the faculty live here?"

"Good Lord, no. There's only twelve or thirteen houses, plus the apartment building has four apartments. Must be close to fifty or sixty faculty and staff and all. A couple of houses come with the job, deans, and higher-ups. I think some of them are saved for the retired Methodist missionaries they get to teach foreign languages, you know, French and Spanish. When they finish twenty or thirty years over in some foreign place, the Methodist church finds a place for them back in the States if they need it, or something. I'm Baptist, so I don't really know the details. I know their pastors are assigned, not selected by the churches. The rest of the housing is sort of first come, first serve. The college rents them for less than going rate, but the problem with it is you never own it. You get to retirement and you don't really have any place to go since you can't sell it and buy someplace else like your sister is doing. Miss Candice had been in her apartment for, like, thirty years. I guess they would have let her keep renting it if she retired, but I don't know that."

Henry had pulled off onto the grass in the middle of the loop.

"Which one is it?"

"In the apartment building, upper floor, on the left. Can you get up one flight of stairs?"

"I'll manage."

They got out, and Alan stared at a brick building with a Southern-style columned entrance porch. Two stories, with four windows on each side of the entrance, window air-conditioners in the slightly larger windows nearest the middle. Alan straightened out his cane and they went across the road. Just inside the door was a hallway, one side filled with stairs to the upper floor. Alan had to climb the steps using only his good leg to move up a step, putting as much weight on the cane as on his other leg when his good leg was moving from step to step, but he got there eventually.

There was still a strip of police tape over the door on the left of the hall. Henry took out a key and unlocked the deadbolt lock. Then he lifted the tape so Alan could enter. Alan stopped in the doorway when he noticed the damage to the doorframe where a chain lock had been ripped out of the wood.

"You see, that's one of the things that makes this case so tough. Both the deadbolt and the chain lock were locked. All the windows were locked from the inside too. Twist locks, not springs. No windows were broken, no signs of ladders on the sills, no footprints on the ground under the windows ten feet below, not even any access to the attic from anywhere except in the hallway. How did the killer get out? There's no way she could have locked the door herself after getting stabbed thirty-two times. And why would she want to?"

"How did you get in?"

"Her neighbor across the hall had a key to the deadbolt. Then he kicked the door in. That's how the chain lock got torn out of the frame. He's the one who discovered the body. It's not unusual around here to give a key to your neighbor so they can watch your place when you're gone, check the gas, let repairmen in, take care of things. He said he smelled a bad smell in the hall, you know, like blood and urine and feces, and tracked it to this apartment. He knocked and tried to rouse Miss Candice, got no response, checked that her car was in the parking lot, and came back and tried again. He said normally he would have assumed she had just walked across the football field out back to the campus, but it was between semesters and a Sunday, so everything would have been closed. He got his key and unlocked the deadbolt but couldn't get in because of the chain lock. But he could see in a little, and saw her foot, so he called the police and then kicked his way in. She was right there, bled out and dead for about a day."

Alan took a couple of steps into the room and saw the old-fashioned chalk outline still on the floor and the bloodstains all around it. He noticed a picture in a frame on the top of a book-case and leaned in closer to examine it.

"This her?"

"Yeah, probably thirty years ago."

Alan saw a picture of a thin young woman in a plain dress with a much older man beside her. She had short, almost masculine, sandy hair and big glasses.

"I think that's her father beside her. That's about the only picture of people in the place. There are some that look like places she traveled, but no people in them."

"What's the scar on her lip?"

"Oh, she had a cleft palate as a child. An operation fixed it, but, you know, there was still the scar. She wasn't a looker any way you cut it. Everybody liked her, but nobody *really* liked her, if you know what I mean."

"I think I get the idea."

Alan moved through the apartment. The colors were mostly tans and beiges, the furniture mostly twenty to thirty years old or older. There were lots of bookcases with various novels and classics of English literature, including some of the more modern works that would have come up in classes. One shelf seemed to hold a collection of playbills and concert programs.

"She a theatre patron?"

"She was more than that. According to the people I talked to, she would act in the college productions sometimes. Not so much the last few years, but when she was younger. She also played saxophone sometimes in various college music groups. Supposedly it's really hard for a person with a cleft palate to play saxophone, even one that's been fixed, but she did it. I'm not sure how the people in the other apartments felt about that, the practicing and all, but I couldn't find any record of any complaints to the police about her, for anything."

Alan moved on into the kitchen. There was plenty of food in the cabinets and the refrigerator, though some of the items in the fridge were showing their age. Nothing exotic, just what he would have expected of a kitchen in Eastern Kentucky. He moved on into the bedroom and checked the closets. Little old lady clothes stared back at him wherever he looked. A second bedroom ostensibly was a guest room with a double bed, but the reality was a storage room with a bed in it. Boxes and plastic crates made it clear there had been no guests for years. The medicine chest in the bathroom revealed a few over-the-counter pain meds, but no prescriptions. No evidence she ever took anything stronger than Advil. Everything was neat and in its place.

"You checked her cell phone and computer."

"Lots of calls, texts, and emails with other members of the faculty and some of the administrators, mostly about school stuff, a few with various graduates asking for recommendations or just telling her how well they were doing. Social stuff was with other faculty or related to college activities. She did some shopping online. We don't have a lot of big stores around here. It's better than it was now we got the Walmart; people used to drive all the way to Corbin to go grocery shopping sometimes. Corbin's home of the original Kentucky Fried Chicken restaurant, if you're interested in that kind of thing. Started out as a gas station. Colonel Sanders added serving food. He was a Kentucky Colonel, you know, not a military colonel. It's sort of an award thing."

"What did she shop for, online?"

"Oh, clothes mostly. Books occasionally. Shoes a couple of times. I think she had to send those back though. Guess they didn't fit."

"Who was in the building the day she was killed?"

"Well, you see, that's the other part of the problem. As far as we know, nobody."

"Nobody?"

"Well, her, of course. And I guess whoever killed her. But it was after the end of the semester and all the grades were turned in and stuff, but the summer semester, what there is of it, hadn't started. Reverend Marigold, the guy across the hall, teaches the religion classes, was on some kind of retreat at a conference center down in North Carolina. Didn't get back until that night.

Miss Pesce, the history teacher downstairs, was up in Lexington hitting all the malls and catching a movie. She spent the night up there at a Days Inn. Got back on Sunday afternoon to find police all over the building. The downstairs on the other side is Dr. Van Doren. He's biology. He was in the Daniel Boone National Forest with ten students on some kind of field trip for a week. Even the houses on either side of the building were empty that day. Football field out back, open field out front until you get to the other side of the circle. Even if she screamed, wasn't nobody here to hear her."

"You checked on all that?"

"Oh, yeah. So did the State people. They were where they said they were."

"The religion teacher was the only one that got back that day?"

"Yeah. But he said he was tired and just went to bed. Didn't even know if Miss Candice was home. At least, till he got up the next morning and smelled the stink."

Alan crossed over to the window and looked over the air conditioning unit at the open field inside the circle of the street. There were several trees in the various yards that would have blocked any views of the window, as well as prevent any vehicles from getting close to the window. He went to the other rooms and looked out. Behind was the college football and track field. Out the windows at the end of the building was a view of the house next door, but it had no windows facing the apartments.

"And she was killed about nine o'clock on the Saturday, give or take?"

"That's what they ended up with as a time of death. The coroner here is just an old country doctor and he at first said twelve to eighteen hours before. Then one of the State people pointed out that the air conditioning was off; it would have been a good deal warmer in here than the coroner had figured, so the body would have cooled slower. They finally agreed on twenty-four hours, give or take three or four. Still well within the time she should have been alone."

"Why would her air conditioning be off this time of year?"

"Most people turn theirs off if they are going to be gone for any length of time. Saves electric bills with these window units. We don't know if she was fixing to leave or had just got back, but it was off when we got here."

"Did the coroner say anything about what kind of knife it was?"

"Big hunting knife. About an eight-inch blade, maybe two inches wide at the widest. Probably had a hilt. Half the hunters in the county probably have one. I know of at least five stores in town that sell them, and that's just in Barbourville. Used for field dressing whatever animals you kill. That's the best they could say without the actual knife."

"Could they tell from the angle whether the killer was right-handed or left?"

"Right. Probably a man, but possibly a strong woman. Didn't narrow things down a lot."

"No kidding. Financial records?"

"She had an IRA with a couple hundred thousand dollars in it. Checking account, savings account, few thousand in each. Her salary was good for around here, but not much compared to most college professors other places. She would probably have made more if she retired and combined retirement pay with social security. But I guess she wanted to keep on teaching. Not rich by any means, but not hurting. No debts we could find, credit cards all paid up."

"Insurance, heirs?"

"She'd basically outlived the term policy the college provided. No children or other relatives. She was an only child, born to older parents. Her mother died when she was a teen. Father died not long after that picture was taken, I think. Will leaves most of her money to the college, with a few bequests to individuals. Nothing more than a thousand dollars to any one person though. Hardly anything to kill her over."

"Any sign of cancer or other health problems?"

"Autopsy didn't find anything. Doc said she was probably starting to slow down with age, but nothing serious hanging over her head yet. I talked on the phone to a few students from last semester, and they all said she was still sharp as a tack mentally. You see my problem? Nobody was here when she died. The apartment was locked from the inside. But she couldn't have killed herself. And I can't find any reason anybody would want to kill her."

"And yet she's dead."

"And yet she's dead."

"Which means that somebody was here when she died. And that not all the ways in or out were locked from the inside. And that somebody at least thought they had a reason to want her dead."

"But who? And how? And what do I do now?"

"You keep on looking until you find something. Go back over the process. What's the first thing you did after examining the scene?"

"Talked to the man who found the body."

"OK, let's go do that again."

"I think I saw his car in the residents' parking lot. We can knock on his door and see if he's home."

They went back into the hall, with Henry carefully locking the door behind them, and making sure the police tape was firmly in place. Then he crossed the hall and knocked on the door of the other second-floor apartment.

"Reverend Marigold, it's Detective Sloop. Could we speak to you for a minute?"

"Hang on."

After a moment, the door opened, and Alan saw someone who was the opposite of the expectations he had for a religion teacher named Marigold. First, he was younger than expected, probably barely in his thirties. Second, he had obviously pumped a lot of iron and more resembled a smaller version of Arnold Schwarzenegger than a larger version of Jerry Falwell. Third, he was wearing a tight T-shirt, plain white, and jeans.

"Reverend Marigold, this is Detective Brown from Massachusetts. He's consulting with us on the Candice Timm case. We were wondering if we could talk to you for a few minutes."

"Sure. Come in, come in."

They were ushered into the living room, which had Scandinavian-style furniture that couldn't be more than a year or two old. What Alan could see of the rest of the apartment also seemed modern and stylish. The detectives were gestured to sit on the sofa, while the Reverend took a seat in a leather chair across from them.

"Could I get you some coffee, tea, maybe a Coke?"

"No, thank you, Reverend Marigold—"

"Whitney, please."

"Whitney, as Detective Sloop said, I've been asked to review this case. We don't want to take up too much of your time, but since you were the one who found the body, I was hoping you could go over things with me."

"Sure, no problem."

"Good. Thank you. Now, I understand you were out of town on the Saturday before?"

"Yes. I was at Lake Junaluska Conference Center. It's a Methodist retreat center outside Ashville, North Carolina. I was at a conference for ministers and other Methodist clergy. Christian Ethics in Academia."

"Could you please start with when you left there, and, please, don't leave anything out."

"Well, the conference got out after lunch so all the preachers could get home in time to write their Sunday sermons. I talked to a few people after lunch; it was probably between two and two-thirty before I left. Maybe closer to two-thirty. It's almost a three-hour drive-up Highway 25, but there was a traffic jam coming through the Cumberland Gap. Also, I stopped in Middlesboro at that King Chinese Buffet. There's a Chinese restaurant over by the Walmart here in town, but it's not my favorite, so I try to chow down on Chinese when I'm traveling. Lots of veggies, not much grease, you know? Anyway, it was probably seven or after before I got home. By then I was a little tired, and a little sleepy from all the Chinese food; I just unloaded the car, checked my emails, and called it an early night. Probably in bed by nine, nine-thirty."

"And you didn't notice anything about the other apartment when you came in?"

"No. It was quiet, and I was tired, so I just came straight into my place."

"OK, go on. Nothing happened during the night?"

"Nothing that woke me. I was out of it at least until seven."

"And then?"

"I got up, had some coffee, and got dressed for church. I was on my way out when I noticed a bad smell in the hall. At first, I couldn't tell where it was coming from, but I figured I better check on Candice. I knocked on her door but didn't get an answer. I went back into my place. From my back windows, I can see the residents' parking lot. Her car was in her parking place, so I got my key to her apartment, went back to the door and knocked, and called out. There was still no response, so I used my key. I could get the door open a crack, but there was a chain holding it closed. But I could peek through the crack and see her foot on the floor like she was lying down. At that point, I got really worried about her. I had my cell phone, so I called 911 and asked for an ambulance. Then I took a step back and kicked the door as hard as I could several times. I finally got the chain dislodged, then went in to see her lying on the floor with blood and other body stuff everywhere. I mean, it was sickening. It was obvious she was dead, so I told 911 I needed the police, not medics. Then I sort of stood there, not sure what to do or not do, until the police came and asked me to step out of the apartment. I stayed in the hall for a while, then felt like I was getting in the way as all the other police arrived. So, I went back to my apartment. A little while later, Detective Sloop came in to talk to me, and I told him basically what I'm telling you now."

"OK. Tell me about her, the victim."

"Candice? She was a nice lady. I only got here about a year ago, two semesters really, so I didn't know her that well. We didn't socialize except for college functions. She was a good deal older than me. But she was a good neighbor. She had a key to my place just like I had a key to hers, and we let in repairmen or checked on things while the other was away. She was respected as a good teacher at the college, and most of her students liked her. At least that was the impression I had from others."

"What did she do with her free time?"

"I'm not sure I really know. She was well-read, of course, kept up to date on modern literature, so I guess she read a lot. Sometimes I could hear her TV on when I was in the hall. She also played a lot of music, radio, CDs, that kind of thing. I hear she used to play sax and recorder, but I don't remember hearing that myself. She did go to the college events, football and basketball games, plays, that sort of thing. Teaching English requires a lot of grading of essays and tests and things like that, so I'm not sure how much free time she had during the semester. I know she traveled some during breaks, had been to England two or three times."

"Did she have a lot of guests visit her?"

"Well, I'm not sure what you consider a lot, but I'd say not very many. Never any students. Some of the women faculty or spouses of male faculty occasionally. Almost never any men, as far as I know, if that's what you're wondering about. That kind of thing would not be welcomed at this school. She was on several committees and was the faculty sponsor of a couple of student organizations, but that business was done on campus, not here."

"What about you, did you ever visit her?"

"Well, I was in her apartment a few times, if that's what you're asking. I helped her carry some heavy packages up the stairs several times, took them into the apartment. Shifted a couple of pieces of furniture once. I was in there a couple of times when I let repairmen in to work on something, a leaky sink, that kind of thing, while she was out of town."

"Did she go out of town often?"

"We all run to Corbin or up to Lexington occasionally. Thou shalt not live by Walmart alone. I would say she did it less than most. I think she was getting a little afraid of her own driving."

"Your apartment is basically like hers, right? Do you have any idea how the killer could have gotten out of the apartment with the chain lock in place and the windows locked from the inside?"

"None whatsoever. I don't see how it's possible."

"I don't either. Which means it probably didn't happen that way."

"So how . . . ?"

"Whitney, excuse me for asking; it's just the kind of thing a police officer has to do. But, did you ever take steroids?"

"Ah, you see the muscles."

"Well, did you?"

"I have admitted that in my youth there was a short period when I took steroids when I first got into bodybuilding. Maybe six months. I haven't tried to keep that a secret. But as I learned more, I decided they were just too dangerous, too many side effects. After that, it was just pumping iron."

"What got you into bodybuilding?"

"Believe it or not, I was not a healthy child. It wasn't the weakling getting sand kicked in his face stereotype; it was a touch of asthma and just generally not being very healthy. I thought getting stronger might help me. Turned out I was right. My health did improve. That got me hooked, and I just kept going to see how far I could go."

"Ever compete in contests?"

"Little local stuff. Nothing serious. But looking good makes me feel good about myself."

"Where were you before you came to Union?"

"Am I under suspicion of something?"

"Just curious. I'm known for being thorough."

"I was a minister at a church in West Virginia."

"How long were you there?"

"Just a year. Before that, I was in grad school earning my master's of divinity degree."

"I understand Methodist ministers are assigned to churches."

"Yes. By the area bishops."

"Were you assigned here?"

"No, I applied to the college for this position."

"Why leave the ministry after just one year?"

"Let's just say it wasn't what I was expecting."

"How so?"

"People weren't interested in hearing new ideas; they were interested in hearing their own ideas approved of."

"I see. And if I called your Bishop in West Virginia, is that what he would tell me?"

"He would tell you that some members of the congregation expressed dissatisfaction with my ministry. But I could have been assigned to another church. It was my decision to move into academia."

"And how are you doing here?"

"Well, I haven't been fired yet."

"But there are, shall we say, dissatisfied members of the college?"

"I hope not. I guess I have made a few rookie teaching mistakes. You can't make everybody happy all of the time, but I try not to hurt any feelings."

"And what's your social life like, Whitney?"

"I'm not sure I want to keep answering these questions."

"Humor me."

"Well, frankly, I haven't had much of a social life here. Part of that is being a new teacher. There's a lot more preparation the first time through a course, and all the courses are new to me. Four new courses each semester, eight sets of lesson plans to prepare over the year, background reading and research, tests to develop and grade, essays to read. Doesn't leave a lot of time for other things. I try to take part in the college activities, as do most of the faculty. That's about all the social life I have time for. I'm not complaining; I'm happy to be here. But that's just the life of a college teacher."

"No dating?"

"Not much time, even fewer opportunities, if you know what I mean."

"Even with the big biceps?"

"Not many women want to be a minister's wife. And I don't blame them."

"No, I can see that. Tell me, Whitney, would you be willing to come with us over to the clinic and provide a blood sample, just to prove you're off the steroids."

"Somehow I don't think that's a good idea. At least not without talking to a lawyer first. You act like you think I killed Candice."

"Oh, I think you did. And I think I know how you did it. I just don't know why, yet. I'm going to start with a call to that Bishop, then talk to the faculty and students about you, maybe even talk to some of the people at that conference and your old church and at your grad school when you were there. Sooner or later I will find what I need."

"I think you better leave now."

"Yes, I suppose we should."

Alan stood, followed by Henry, and hobbled to the door.

"Oh, don't leave town, Whitney. That's such a cliché thing to say, but still . . ."

Alan slowly worked his way back down the stairs and crossed to the car. They got in, and Henry turned to Alan.

"He did it? Killed Miss Candice?"

"That would be my guess."

"How? How do you know?"

"I'll tell you in a minute. There's only one road out of here, right?"

"Yeah."

"OK, drive out, then park somewhere we can watch the exit without being seen from the apartment building."

"You think he's going to skip?"

"I would be a little surprised if he didn't. He doesn't impress me as the kind that would try to brazen this out. And then we would know for sure."

Henry started the car and drove the rest of the way around the circle. At the entrance to the road, he turned left onto Johnson Lane, then quickly right onto North Broadway. There, he did a U-turn and took up a position where they could see the exit from College Park Drive.

"OK, now explain this to me, and remember, I'm just a hick from the hills, so make it simple."

"Come on, Henry, don't put yourself down like that. You just have to look at things a little differently. First of all, if it's impossible for someone to have killed her and then gotten out of the locked apartment, then that's not what happened. So what could have happened? Either the apartment was not locked when her killer left, or she wasn't killed Saturday morning."

"So which was it?"

"Both, I think. Let's say she wasn't dead when Whitney got home, which may have been a little earlier than he claimed. He comes up the stairs and Candice comes to her door to say hello or tell him something. She sees him carrying something she shouldn't have seen or she says something she shouldn't have, I'm not sure which. Something that would have ended his academic career or ruined his life somehow."

"Yeah."

"He's back on steroids, and maybe on something else. Something that makes him feel better about himself after basically getting fired from the church and maybe having problems with this job. Anyway, whatever Candice saw or said sets off a steroid rage. Candice goes back into her apartment and locks her door, deadbolt and chain lock. He gets his key and knife, unlocks the deadbolt, and kicks in the chain. He stabs her. He leaves the apartment, goes back to his place, takes off his bloody clothes, showers, changes. During this time, he comes up with a plan. It's actually a good plan. He takes his key and goes back to Candice's apartment and turns down the air conditioner, down to as low a setting as it has. This keeps her body cooler than the coroner expects, making her liver temperature lower than expected. Probably not a huge difference, but I think your country doctor was closer to the truth than the State guys. He locks the apartment and goes back and gets a good night's sleep. Next morning, he gets up early, goes to Candy's apartment, and turns off the air conditioner. He goes back to his apartment, has his coffee, gets dressed for church, goes in the hall, calls 911, unlocks the apartment with his key yet again, then waits for the police to arrive. Tells you he never saw her the night before. At least that fits all the facts as we know them."

Just then, a car pulled out of College Park Drive.

"There he goes."

"Give him a little lead until he gets out of town. We don't want him claiming he was on his way to Walmart or something."

They followed the other car down to College Drive, onto Daniel Boone Drive, and then onto Cumberland Gap Parkway. He turned east, probably headed for the Cumberland Gap, where Kentucky, Virginia, and Tennessee meet and he could get out of Kentucky the fastest. They waited until he was past all the stores and shops along the parkway, then pulled him over in Bimble, an even smaller town just east of Barbourville. He pulled into the driveway of Knox Central High School. Henry got out with his gun drawn and quietly made the arrest. He put on handcuffs, searched Whitney, then put him in the back seat of the patrol car. He then went back to Whitney's car, popped the trunk, and saw two large suitcases and a backpack. He locked Whitney's car and they waited until two more Barbourville police arrived to take possession of Whitney's car. Henry then climbed back into his patrol car.

"He say anything yet?"

"Not a word."

"And I'm not going to until I have a lawyer."

"That's probably smart of you, Whitney, but I don't think it's going to make much difference once Henry here finishes his investigation. A few warrants for a drug screen and searches of your apartment and car, not to mention all those phone calls I mentioned, and he'll find the motive. We already have means and opportunity."

"We'll see about that."

"You and Henry will. I'm driving to Florida with my sister. She says she'll have a spare bedroom down there. I suspect I'll go back to Plymouth for the summer, but I'm thinking Florida may be nice in the winter. My knee aches when it gets cold. They probably have good seafood down there too. Probably not lobster, like in Plymouth, but some good fish. Better than a cold jail cell and sloppy joes in a Kentucky prison."

"Damn you, Detective, damn you."

"Thank you, Whitney; I appreciate the compliment, especially coming from a man of God."

And Henry started the car and drove back to Barbourville.

The Round One

He wasn't supposed to be a detective. He'd never even been a cop. No training, no license. And he certainly didn't look like one. He wasn't really as wide as he was tall, but he sort of looked like it. A round ball of a person. Round face too. Full black beard, and bushy hair. Indeterminate middle age. A bad football lineman badly gone to seed. Not impressive looking at all.

But then, he didn't claim to be a detective either. The sign on the door of his little office in the big, downtown Atlanta office building said, RON WADE, CONSULTANT. It didn't specify what kind of consultant, or what areas he consulted in. Just CONSULTANT. No secretary, no waiting room. Just a little room with a desk, a big desk chair for him, two guest chairs, three computers (each with its own high-speed web connection), and a copier/printer/scanner/fax machine in the corner. No window, just an overhead light, and a desk lamp. Bare bones furnishing, except for the heavily padded and reinforced desk chair that you could barely see when he was sitting in it, and the computers, of course. They were state-of-the-art.

It was enough for him. He was a man of modest expectations. He could have afforded more and bigger since he was actually well-paid for "consulting." And he had lived frugally and invested wisely. No family. But this was enough for him. It was comfortable, manageable. Besides, clients rarely came into the office. Video conferencing, emails, texts, and occasional phone calls took care of most business communication. And most of his work was business; what computers to buy for businesses, what software best fit certain types of businesses, how to make money using computers, how to use money, how to do things more efficiently, how to do more with less.

But occasionally, some other puzzle came in; someone had heard over the grapevine that he might be able to solve a mystery, a puzzle. He liked solving puzzles. That was actually what he was good at. Football had been his ticket to a degree in computer science, despite usually being third string on a second-rate college team. His size had got him that far, but no further. Now, he had to live by his wits. Usually, with the World Wide Web at his disposal, he could find the answer without getting out of his well-padded chair. Most times, somebody else somewhere had already solved that puzzle. The word just hadn't gotten around to everybody yet. Or they had solved a similar puzzle, but nobody had applied the answer to this other question. Lateral thinking, seeing things sideways, usually took care of most quandaries.

Usually, but not always. Once in a while, something else came up. Like the email that came in this morning. All it said was, *$5,000 if you can find the girl.* The sender's URL was a bunch of gibberish that showed intent to hide the source. But it had a bunch of attachments; a copy of a police report, numerous pictures of an apartment, a couple of newspaper stories, a missing person poster. He finished up a report to Mayfair Moving Company on how to track moving pads, which had a nasty habit of disappearing, sent that off by email along with an invoice, and checked his calendar. He had a little time.

By then it was noon, so he went down the elevator to the food court on the ground floor of the office complex. He went to the Chick-fil-A restaurant and ate a salad and drank sweet iced tea. He really didn't eat that much, not anymore, but he was still big. He liked to think he wasn't fat, just big. He had to be strong just to move his body around, but grace was not his middle name. Too much time in that big armchair behind his desk.

Back at that desk, he started opening the email attachments. According to the Decatur, Georgia, police report, a call from the resident office manager of the Adie Apartment Complex had come in at 10:08 a.m. on Monday, June 19. The office manager, Rosie Roberts, reported that she had received a complaint from a resident on the sixth floor that her next-door neighbor had played the Beatles's *White Album* at a volume audible across apartments all night long, over and over, despite bangs on the wall. The complaining resident had then left for work, but the manager had called up to the offending apartment several times without getting a response.

Finally, the manager had gone up to the sixth floor, easily located the apartment that was the source of the offending music, and knocked repeatedly; again getting no response. The manager had gone back to her office and gotten the office key to that apartment and unlocked the door, calling out to the unresponding resident. But the door was blocked by a security chain. That was not standard apartment equipment. In fact, security chains were forbidden in case the maintenance staff ever had to enter the apartment in an emergency. But through the crack allowed by the chain, the manager could see the apartment was in disarray, items broken and scattered across the floor.

She put in an emergency call to the maintenance man on duty and waited in the hall for him to arrive. While she waited, she kept calling into the apartment through the crack in the door. When the maintenance man arrived, he couldn't figure out a way to unlock the security chain from outside, so he finally just used a big screwdriver to pry it off the doorframe.

On entering, they found household items scattered and broken, a white coffee table shattered and collapsed on the floor. The bed in the bedroom was in disarray, sheets thrown back, blanket on the floor. In the bathroom, the shower curtain was partly torn down. In the kitchen, the refrigerator door was open, food had been spilled on the floor, cabinets were partly emptied, and cans and boxes littered the countertops and floor. In all the rooms, drawers were left open and some contents were scattered, closets standing open, and many clothes were pulled from their hangers. But nobody was there, dead or alive.

Once they determined there was no medical emergency, they backed out of the apartment and called the police. The manager waited in the hall until a uniformed officer arrived. It was the officer who had called for detectives. Detectives Anthony Hall and Roscoe Jenkins had arrived by eleven a.m., surveyed the scene, and called for a photographer and CSI unit. Then they finally turned off the old-fashioned CD player, which had been set on repeat. The pictures attached to the email were those taken by the police photographer. Basically, they showed a sixth-floor, one-bedroom apartment in a middle rent-level apartment complex in downtown Decatur, Georgia. An apartment that was all messed up.

Interviewing the resident manager back in her office where she had access to her lease records, the detectives determined that the missing resident was a Miss Susan Ann Carter, twenty-seven years old, employed at the Barnes and Williams Accounting firm in downtown Atlanta; and her emergency contact was her father, a William J. Carter of Medford, OR.

Phone calls to Susan's employer revealed that she worked a flex-time schedule of nine-hour days, five days one week and four days the next. This Monday was her off day, so nobody had missed her yet. Yes, her desk still had its normal equipment and supplies, plus the few personal items she could cram into the cubicle allotted to a junior accountant. Coworkers reported seeing her last on Friday at quitting time and not noticing anything unusual, though she was quiet and kept to herself normally.

A call to her father determined that he was an administrator in the Oregon Unemployment Office, that Susan's mother had died when Susan was a teenager, that she had no siblings, and that she had last spoken to her father the prior weekend but had not reported any problems or worries. The father said he would fly to Atlanta as soon as possible.

Ordering the apartment manager to preserve any security videos in the building, the detectives returned to the apartment. There, they determined that the sliding glass door to the balcony was locked from the inside, both the glass door and the screen door outside it. The balcony was only about three feet deep, and there were wall projections between apartments that stuck out several feet and were smooth with no handholds or other ways to go between apartments on the outside. However, the detectives reported that it might be possible for an intruder to climb up from the balcony below. But, the balcony doors had been thumb-latched from the inside, and they had already heard about the trouble the manager had getting into the apartment because of the security chain—which could only be closed from the inside. At this point, even the dispassionate police report seemed puzzled.

The detectives also found Susan's purse on the floor under a throw pillow from the sofa. Her keys, apartment key fob, phone, driver's license, employee ID, several credit cards, and thirty-seven dollars in cash were inside. Her phone showed no calls since her call to her father over a week ago. The contacts list only had the number for apartment maintenance and five of the people at her office. There were no pictures. Her passport and checkbook were found in a half-open drawer in the bedroom. Her checkbook showed a balance of several hundred dollars, but no big withdrawals. Her laptop computer was also found but it was broken badly, especially the hard drive, and no information could be obtained. There were two suitcases and a backpack in the closet, and no clothes seemed to be missing, just scattered everywhere. The only picture of Susan they could find was the one on her license. Information from the license and a call to the DMV produced information about Susan's car. It was a five-year-old Toyota Camry, white, with gray cloth upholstery. One of the uniformed officers quickly found the car in the apartment building's parking garage, undisturbed. Detective Jenkins took the keys from Susan's purse out to the car, opened the doors and trunk, found nothing notable, but called the CSI unit out to check it with a fine-tooth comb.

Next, the detectives and a couple of the uniformed officers began canvasing the other apartments. Most residents were at work, but the few at home had little to add. Yes, many of them had seen Susan in the halls. A few admitted to exchanging "hellos" in passing or knowing which apartment she lived in. No one admitted to knowing her better than that or ever having gone into her apartment. Susan evidently never attended the social activities the complex occasionally sponsored.

Back at the manager's office, she reported that the management company had changed recently, and she had only been there two months; she and all her staff were new to the building and didn't know many of the renters, especially if they hadn't had any maintenance problems or lease issues. Susan had her rent automatically paid by her bank's bill-paying service, her lease was due to run for another six months, and she had not reported any problems with the apartment. The manager gave the detectives a memory stick with the security camera recordings for the previous seven days.

At this point, the police report seemed to indicate a noticeable increase in concern on the part of the detectives. A BOLO had already gone out, but now the picture on the license was scanned and distributed. The detectives dropped the security recordings at the police department for others to review and headed downtown to Susan's office, evidently giving up on eating any lunch that day.

Interviews with Susan's supervisor and several coworkers described a quiet but competent worker, well-trained in accounting and very good with the new accounting software and technology. She usually ate lunch at her desk, dressed conservatively (as did they all), and kept any social life she might have had to herself. None of the males remarked about her looks or personality, which the detectives found a little surprising. The women said she was plain but could have been pretty with a little effort. "You know how accountants are, all about the numbers, not good socializers," was a quote one of the detectives had written down.

But everybody said she had been a very good accountant,

working with several of the senior accountants on a wide variety of projects involving banks, investment firms, department stores, and large legal firms, among others. But nobody knew anything about what she did after five o'clock.

The detectives tried to reach her father again, but he evidently was in the air somewhere between Oregon and Georgia. Back at the apartment, they went through everything more thoroughly now that the CSI team was finished. No church bulletins or nightclub coasters, no mail beyond bills and mass mailings, no signs of a life outside her job. She did have a Spectrum cable box and a Roku module on her TV. There were a few romance paperbacks, but no other books.

The preliminary CSI oral report was that they found no blood in the apartment, no semen on the sheets, and hundreds of fingerprints, but probably all from the same person, who the detectives assumed was Susan herself.

It was now early evening, so the detectives went back to question the people who had not been home earlier, but the results were the same. No one seemed to know much about Susan or who she hung out with or what could have happened to her. The apartment directly above Susan's was vacant, but the one directly below held a young couple who said they didn't know Susan, had been home both Saturday and Sunday night, and thought they would have noticed if anybody had climbed over their balcony unless they were very, very quiet.

The police report then skipped to the morning of the next day. When the detectives reported for duty, they were given a report on the security tapes. Susan could be seen entering the building Friday night at about six o'clock, coming in the side door nearest the MARTA subway station in downtown Decatur, using her key fob for entry. She was on the video of the elevator going up to the sixth floor. There were no security cameras in the hallways, so all they knew was that she entered the building and went up in the elevator. There was no video showing her leaving. Lots of other people came and went, mostly residents using their key fobs, but some with guests accompanying them. It was a big building, almost two hundred apartments, so many people in the videos were unidentified.

Susan's father was also waiting to see them. They had very little to tell him except his daughter was still missing. They asked him if he had had any contact with her or knew any names of friends or groups they could talk to about Susan. He had no suggestions. He never talked to his daughter about her social life. They had grown apart after her mother died. When Susan went away to school at the University of Georgia, far from Oregon, he had taken that as a sign she wanted to start her own life, separate from him, and hadn't pressed her on anything she didn't volunteer about herself. But she was a serious person, not prone to partying. Never used drugs. She had earned very good grades and had several offers of employment after completing her accounting degree with a minor in French.

At this point, the police report started to become sparse. They had tried to find a way to lock a security chain from the outside but had failed. They had surveyed the building from outside to see if there was a way to scale it from the ground, but the first floor was higher than the rest of the floors and had no balcony railings like the floors above, so someone would have to have used a ladder or started from a floor above the first floor. All the apartment residents below Susan's apartment denied anyone starting the climb from their apartments. Someone suggested that an intruder could have climbed down two levels from the roof, but no one could figure out how they could have gotten away with a body or reluctant victim. They searched the roof and ground outside the building but found no evidence of anything.

The final CSI report just confirmed the preliminary report. No sightings were reported, despite publicity on TV and missing person posters in the area around her apartment and office. There was no activity in her bank account. The detectives quickly ran out of leads to follow. It was as if a person nobody really knew had vanished into thin air in the middle of a locked apartment.

After a week, her father had to go back to Oregon. The case was still open, officially, but now, all this time later, they were waiting on a break, on something else to happen somewhere.

At this point, Ron finished reading. He examined the attached photos, magnifying them on his highest-resolution screen. It almost seemed like too much disorder to him, purposeless, not the result of fighting or searching, but he couldn't be certain. *Keep an open mind*, he told himself. He reviewed the missing person poster and the newspaper clippings but they didn't tell him anything new.

By now, it was five o'clock; he copied the attachments to his laptop, logged out of his desktop computers, and went back to the food court for supper. This time, he went to Willy's for a veggie burrito and taco chips plus more sweet tea. Sitting at the table, he reviewed the police report on his laptop. After supper, he went down the world's longest escalator to the MARTA station, took the north line to Lindbergh Station, changed to the Gold Line, and went north one more station to Lenox Station. He walked across East Paces Ferry Road at the crosswalk, past the first apartment complex, and into the second complex. He stopped to pick up his mail, but it was all circulars and ads so he threw them away. His apartment was only on the third floor, but he took the elevator. His building was in the upscale Lenox area, but it was not the most luxurious. It was also one of the older apartment buildings in the area, so not as expensive as one would expect. Not like the new high-rise buildings not far away. Besides, he only had a one-bedroom apartment. It was substantially bigger than Susan's appeared to be, but not huge. Besides, his view was of the apartment complex on the other side, which reduced his rent compared to the other, more scenic, side of the building. Enough for him. Inside, he relaxed in an armchair, reviewed the police report one more time, considered his next steps, then spent the rest of the evening reading Noam Chomsky's book, *The Logical Structure of Linguistic Theory*.

The next morning, he showered and dressed, then reversed

his course from yesterday to take MARTA downtown. He stopped in the food court and ate breakfast at Metro Café Diner (two eggs, scrambled; grits; and orange juice). He stopped at Caribou Coffee for a large black coffee and took that back to his office. He booted up his computers and read the electronic edition of the *Atlanta Journal-Constitution* before opening his email. There were several new emails, but he dealt with them in fifteen minutes and turned to the missing person case.

First, he got Susan's father's email address from the police report and emailed him.

> *Dear Mr. Carter,*
>
> *My name is Ron Wade. I am a Private Consultant. I have been engaged to find your daughter, Susan Ann Carter. I have reviewed the police report, but I have a few questions. Have you had any contact with Susan or with anyone who knew Susan since her disappearance? Do you know if Susan did any traveling outside Atlanta since her college graduation? Did she have any hobbies or other interests through which she might have met people outside her employment? Thank you for any information you can provide.*

Next, he emailed Detective Hall.

> *Detective Hall,*
>
> *My name is Ron Wade. I am a Private Consultant. I have been engaged to find Susan Ann Carter. My information is that you are the lead investigator on that missing person case. I have reviewed the police report. I am sure you are busy, but it might help my inquiry substantially if I could review the apartment building security tapes. Any assistance along those lines would be appreciated. I'm sure it is a large file, but I have a Dropbox account which should be sufficient. Thank you for your assistance.*

Then he provided information on how to forward the file to him.

As he waited for responses, he checked the status of his invoices and payments, made sure his bills were being paid automatically, and sent reminders to clients who were late paying their bills. Just as he finished his bookkeeping, Susan's father replied.

> *Mr. Wade, I would be happy for any information you can provide about my daughter. Her disappearance has just about destroyed me. Mostly it is the not knowing what happened, whether she is dead or alive, and imagining all the things that she could be going through. Please help any way you can.*
>
> *As for your questions, no, I have not heard anything from my daughter or anyone who knew my daughter. My last contact with her was more than a week before her disappearance.*
>
> *She has traveled a little bit. She always came home to Oregon for Christmas, but otherwise didn't have money for much outside the Atlanta area, or accumulated time off from her job for anything extensive. She did fly to the Bahamas last summer for a week, about the middle of July, mostly to snorkel and see the sights. I think she was planning another trip for later this summer, but we hadn't discussed where or when.*
>
> *As for hobbies, outside of jogging to stay in shape, I am not aware of anything. She spent a lot of time on computers, even outside of work, but she said a lot of that was keeping up with new accounting software and other things related to financial stuff. She really didn't talk to me much about her life outside accounting. She is very smart but seemed to be content to focus on her career.*
>
> *I'm sorry I can't be more help. I just don't know what else to do. Please let me know if I can help you in any way at all.*

Ron was pondering this information when a ping informed him something had appeared in his Dropbox file. It turned out to be the file from the detective with all the security recordings. He spent the rest of the morning going through the videos, fast-forwarding through the recording to each entrance to and exit from the building, beginning at about three in the morning on Thursday. He didn't try to identify any individuals, just counted entrances and exits until the end of the recording, when the manager had stopped the system to make a copy for the detectives. It didn't prove anything, but it made him feel a little better when the number of people entering equaled the number of people exiting, not counting all the police. It was enough of a cheerful thought that he went to Firehouse Subs in the food court and got a ham and cheese sub for lunch.

Back at the office afterward, he obtained online access, perhaps not totally legally, to the flight manifests of all the flights from Hartsfield-Jackson airport to anywhere in the Bahamas, and did a search for Susan Carter in July of last year. She had flown on Delta 638 to Nassau at 8:17 a.m., Saturday, July 13, and returned the following Sunday, a week later. This would have avoided all the Fourth of July crowds and probably included one of her Mondays off.

Next, he looked for the lists of passengers flying to the Bahamas on the day that Susan disappeared. This was hundreds of people. First, he eliminated all the males and people flying on a child's ticket. Then he deleted all the people where there were two or more people with the same last name flying together. It was still a long list, ninety-seven women, to be exact, but maybe somewhat manageable.

By the time he was done, he had worked overtime. It was almost six o'clock when he settled on a final list of possibilities. And, of course, none of them were "Susan A. Carter." But it was the start of a possibility. Saving the next step, he went down to the food court for supper, hitting up the Farmer's Basket for meatloaf, mac and cheese, fried okra, and black-eyed peas, but declining the cornbread to save calories.

Then it was back to his apartment and an evening of sitting on his balcony, watching the parking lot as people came and went, considering the possibilities. By the morning, he was more certain.

The next step was definitely more sensitive. The Bahamas were known for their deliberately lax banking laws. Money could be hidden in Bahamian banks where the IRS and other regulators would never know. It wasn't as Wild West as it had been at one time, but who owned which accounts or how much was in them was still not something the banks willingly made public. Knowing that he was looking for accounts opened July 15–19, helped, but getting in and out of all the major banks in the Bahamas without setting off all kinds of alarms would be dangerous. He decided to come at it sideways.

He realized that one of the new accounts might have come with a credit card. Which meant it might be for sale on the Dark Web. Which meant he could search there for a name and an account opening date that matched a name that was on one of the flight rosters for June 19 to the Bahamas. It took most of the day. He even skipped lunch. But he finally found a match. Now he had a name.

Back in the airline's manifests, he checked for that name on June 19. There it was. Erica Smith had flown from Atlanta to Nassau on the morning of June 19. The next day, she continued on to Orly Airport in Paris by way of Kennedy Airport in New York, bought another ticket at Orly, and went on to Nicosia, Cypress. If Erica Smith had left Cypress by air, it had not been within a month of arrival.

Ron sat in his office for the rest of the day, quietly considering the possibilities. He thought he now knew what had happened, but he had very little real evidence. He grew hungry and realized it was quitting time. He wanted a quiet meal, so he closed his office and went downstairs to Hsu's Gourmet Chinese for Kung Pao Chicken. Having missed lunch, he was still hungry, so he went on to Planet Smoothie for dessert, selecting a Road Runner that had lots of different kinds of berries.

Back at his apartment, Ron tried reading a collection of e. e. cummings's poetry. That usually cheered him up, but he was having trouble concentrating on it. Somehow, balloon men whistling far and wee couldn't distract him from thinking about Susan. He was almost sure he knew what she had done but he was having trouble understanding why. She had been on course for a successful career as an accountant, already reasonably well paid, nice apartment. Yes, she seemed very much the introvert, but weren't a lot of people? Hadn't she chosen her life as much as anyone could?

The next morning, after the usual breakfast at Metro Café, Ron looked up a couple of phone numbers from his case notes. Some things you did by email or text, but some things you did by phone. The first call was to Susan's supervisor at the accounting firm, a Mr. Adam Ross.

"This is Adam Ross."

"Mr. Ross, my name is Ron Wade. I'm a private consultant hired to find one of your former employees, Susan Carter. I was wondering if I could ask you just a couple of quick questions?"

"Yes, Mr. Wade. We are all very curious about what happened to Susan. She was a good accountant. How can I help?"

"I was wondering if you have a standard procedure you follow when an employee unexpectedly leaves your company?"

"Yes, of course. We immediately did a full review of all the accounts that Susan had worked on during the previous year. And I can assure you that all of those books balanced perfectly."

"What about accounts from previous years? Or clients you handle where your company has access to their software or financial systems, even if Susan didn't work on those?"

"Everything is audited yearly, so any problems would be detected."

"And were any problems detected?"

"Mr. Wade, I'm not at liberty to discuss that over the phone with a person who I don't know anything about."

"I'll take that as a yes."

"Take it any way you want."

"I assume your company has liability insurance?"

"Of course."

"Mr. Ross, you can save me a little time by just telling me, have your liability insurance rates gone up lately?"

"Mr. Wade, this phone call is over."

And Mr. Ross hung up. Ron smiled a little, having enjoyed that.

His next call went to the Adie Apartments office manager, Rosie Roberts.

"Adie Apartments, where fun lives in Decatur, how can I help you?"

"I need to speak to Miss Roberts."

"This is she."

"Miss Roberts, my name is Ron Wade. I am a private consultant employed to find one of your former tenants, Susan Carter."

"Yes, that was a mess."

"If I could ask you just a question or two?"

"Sure, fire away."

"I was wondering if you were showing vacant apartments the day before Susan disappeared?"

"Yeah, sure. I was in the office that day. I guess I showed apartments to six or seven prospects."

"Did you show the vacant apartment directly above Susan's apartment?"

"Uh, let's see. Let me think. Uh, yeah, I did. It was late in the day, just before we closed the office for the day."

"Do you remember anything about the person you showed it to?"

"Oh, wow, you're testing my memory."

"Anything at all?"

"Uh, I think it was a woman. Yeah, a young woman, blond, longish hair. I remember her now because she had a really great figure and I thought she must really attract the men if you know what I mean."

"Yes, anything else?"

"No, not really. She just looked all around the apartment,

opened and closed all the doors, looked for the cable outlets, standard stuff. She didn't rent it though. Never saw her again. I could look up the basic info she had to fill out. I think we still have that card. We sent her a follow-up email and stuff."

"No, thank you. I don't think that will be necessary. Thank you for your help, Miss Roberts."

"Yeah, sure. I hope you aren't blaming the Adie for anything that happened to Susan."

"No, no."

"Great."

"Thank you again."

"Yeah, sure."

And Ron hung up the phone, wondering why a company would hire someone like that to represent them. By now, it was obvious what had happened, but he needed to confirm a few details. The rest of the morning was spent researching insurance companies that sold liability insurance to businesses, especially accounting firms, then reviewing any notices or warnings about types of problems to be on the lookout for. He also got into a few accounting association websites and read any bulletins they might have sent out to association members lately. One warning seemed to appear in several places a few weeks after Susan disappeared. It took a little research to figure out exactly what was being warned against, but once he got the idea, Ron respected the ingenuity.

Lunch was a gyro plate at Great Wraps and sweet tea before heading quickly back to his computers. The afternoon was less successful. He was able to discover what "Erica" had charged on the American Express she had gotten in the Bahamas almost a year ago, which was as he expected. But tracking her after she landed in Cyprus didn't work out. He didn't know when or how or even if she left the island, though he was pretty sure she had and where she had gone. But she was traveling under another name now, with other bank accounts. Finally, he had to decide what he was willing to do to track her. What he decided was to go to supper and deal with it tomorrow.

He decided a little celebration was still in order, so he went to the lower floor of the food court to get to Gus's Fried Chicken. He treated himself to a half chicken and added mac and cheese to the automatic slaw and baked beans, then threw in a piece of chess pie for dessert. That indeed made it an occasion.

Back at his apartment, he got everything in order in his mind and decided the only real question left was why she did it. He couldn't understand. She had worked so hard to get where she was, avoiding so many of the temptations that accompany college and being independent afterward. He considered his own success in life. He couldn't imagine what would make him change his life for something totally different. Nevertheless, he slept well, went for his usual breakfast the next morning, read the *AJC* newspaper online back at his office, and began composing his report.

Dear sir or madam,

As best I have been able to determine, Susan Ann Carter is probably alive and well. This is what I believe happened according to the evidence. During her employment with Barnes and Williams Accounting, she acquired certain information about the financial transaction software being used by one or more of the clients of her firm, though probably not one that she worked with directly. Barnes and Williams, understandably, are not providing details of how she accessed that information, but I am sure Susan must have had access to the software that processed financial transactions at some point.

Prior to her trip to the Bahamas last summer, she obtained the birth certificate of someone else, someone who was born in Oregon on or near her birthday and birthplace but later died. These documents are available from the Vital Records Office in Oregon for a modest fee if you have certain basic information that can be obtained from public records. Using this real document and some other materials readily available on the World Wide Web, she was able to create enough of a fake identity to open at least two bank accounts while in the Bahamas. One of those accounts provided a credit card, which she used to purchase a blond wig, padded bra, and perhaps other materials to create a disguise.

Back in Atlanta, using the information she had acquired at work, she evidently modified the financial processing software of the unidentified firm or firms. It was out-of-date, having not been updated to deal with this well-known manipulation. Basically, Susan reprogramed the software so that whenever it processed a transaction that resulted in a fraction of a cent difference after the calculation (such as when charging fees or dividing money between multiple accounts), instead of rounding off the calculation in favor of one account or the other and giving the extra fraction of a cent to one client or the other, it deposited the fractions of a cent in one of her accounts in the Bahamas. Since a whole cent was never missing from any account of a transaction, this would have gone undetected until the next audit, which was scheduled for July of this year. This may not sound like a lot of money, but with a financial institution processing hundreds of thousands of transactions daily, over almost a year, it would have added up to probably hundreds of thousands of dollars.

In June of this year, before the audit could start, Susan disappeared. It appears what actually happened is that sometime during the week before she left, Susan purchased a mountaineering rope, a couple of pieces of climbing gear, and a security chain for her apartment. The day before she left, donning her disguise, she went down to the apartment building and asked the relatively new manager to show her the vacant apartment that was directly above hers. While examining this apartment, she unlocked the doors to the balcony without the knowledge of the manager.

That evening, under the cover of the music on her CD player, she installed the security chain, trashed her apartment, locked the balcony door from outside, probably using thin wires with a loop put in place as each door was closed, then removing the wire or other such device. Carrying only her disguise and documents for her new identity, she climbed from her balcony to the balcony above, opened the unlocked doors, and spent the rest of the night in the vacant apartment.

The next morning, during the period when many people were leaving early for work and before the police arrived, she put her disguise on, walked out of the vacant apartment unnoticed, leaving it unlocked. The manager probably did not notice the door not being locked until the apartment was shown again much later and then did not connect it to Susan's disappearance. Nor did anyone notice a blond, well-built woman leaving the building, getting on MARTA, and riding to the airport to get a plane to the Bahamas.

In the Bahamas, she probably closed all her accounts, taking most of the money in bearer bonds or other untraceable currency. She then flew to Paris the next day, changed planes, and went to Nicosia, Cyprus. While I have not been able to verify it, I believe she either had another false identity prepared or was able to acquire one in Cyprus. Under this new identity, I believe she opened new, confidential bank accounts and deposited the money. It is possible she may still be in Cyprus, but I consider it more likely she has moved on to France or perhaps another country where French is the official language.

To locate her now would be very difficult, involving significant risk, both to me and to her. I would have to obtain access to banking and travel information that is generally well protected, possibly bending some regulations. It would also place me in the tricky legal position of having information about the identity and whereabouts of a felon.

In addition, if I did find her, it might create an electronic trail that the authorities could follow to locate Susan. And if I did provide that information to you, and you contacted her, you might expose her identity as well.

Since I did not find Susan's specific location or enable you to contact her, I do not expect to receive the stated fee. If you wish me to continue my search in order to find where she is presently, please let me know.

He reread the email, thought if there was anything else he needed to say, then hit SEND. He then turned to his inbox and looked to see what other projects might have come his way to occupy his mind.

Later that afternoon, the reply came.

Dear Mr. Wade, thank you for your email. I appreciate receiving the information you sent. It is somewhat of a relief, as well as a bit of a disappointment. Please do not, I repeat, DO NOT, continue your search for Susan. At this point, I think the best thing is to just let her go. That is certainly not the outcome I was hoping for but is certainly much better than most of the alternatives, all things considered. I have deposited your fee. Thank you again for your prompt attention to this matter.

Ron checked his bank and saw the $5,000 had been processed. He leaned back in his big chair for a moment, considered how much mystery was left to Susan Carter, then returned to his new project.

Acknowledgments

Special thanks to Jim Gray, my expert on aviation and detective stories, who gives the best and most detailed comments. Thanks also to Rich and Kelly Vandever for their expertise on guns. As usual, thanks to Kathy and Elizabeth for putting up with me.

About the Author

David Davis wrote a science fiction novel entitled *The Mistakes*, published by Kohler Books in 2020, and *Seven Heretical Sermons*, published by BookLogix in 2023. In addition, he has had seventeen plays produced, including productions in New York and Hollywood. He has also had several poems, magazine features, and scholarly articles published. He earned a PhD in Theatre and is a member of the Dramatists Guild and Working Title Playwrights. He has worked as a physics and math teacher, actor, head of three college theatre programs, technical writer, editor, and health communications specialist. He currently lives in Atlanta, Georgia, with his wife, Kathy, and has one daughter, Elizabeth.

Other Books by David Davis

The Mistakes

Seven Heretical Sermons

Heartspan

Compiled Poems, 1957-2022

www.ingramcontent.com/pod-product-compliance
Lightning Source LLC
Chambersburg PA
CBHW030425120726
47903CB00003B/812